'I don't imagine the great Damian St. Clair will be thrown by a fashion plate —or will he? They say he's not unobservant of women,' declared Siri as she prepared for that all-important audition with the great conductor. How would she make out with the famous Damian as a singer—and as a woman?

THE LOVE THEME

BY

MARGARET WAY

MILLS & BOON LIMITED
17-19 FOLEY STREET
LONDON W1A 1DR

First published 1974

This edition 1974

© Margaret Way 1974

ISBN 0 263 71597 3

*Made and Printed in Great Britain by
Richard Clay (The Chaucer Press), Ltd., Bungay, Suffolk*

CHAPTER ONE

IT rained the day of the auditions. Not just a steady downpour, but an unheralded deluge flung out of the heavens wholesale. Siri pressed her nose up against the window pane, seeing nothing but silvery cascades of water, each pane a miniature waterfall, and then the frosted circle of her breath upon the glass. Why did it have to be wet and cold? Could there be a less auspicious start to the morning? She threw herself back on the lemon eiderdown, then snuggled down under the blankets, curling her toes in kittenish pleasure. Oh, to be rich and lie late every morning of winter!

She drifted off into a thrilling daydream ... She was imagining the audience had come to their feet for a standing ovation:

'Bravo! ... bravissimo!'

'For heaven's sake, Siri, you can't lie there any longer!' Where did the voice come from? Siri opened her eyes to reality. Her aunt Charlotte's face swam into focus.

'Come on now, Siri. I refuse to let you go off without breakfast. It simply won't do!'

Siri shivered and tried, ineffectually, to retrieve the eiderdown, but Charlotte was quicker, grabbing it and tucking it implacably under her arm. She watched her niece sit up groaning and protesting as she had done every morning since bright autumn had passed into winter. Charlotte gazed at her fondly. How lovely Siri was, and how like her dear, dead Catherine—Catherine, of the dark hair, great shadowy eyes and thick creamy skin.

Siri's long glossy pigtail hung over one shoulder, inky black and completely resistant to curl. Charlotte remembered the struggles they had to fashion some sort of curl for a speech day or a prizegiving, or some such occasion. The curls had just refused to stay curled for more than ten minutes, and even less if it was raining! Yet Siri's eyes were more remarkable than Cat's. They were the same smoky grey, set in the same density of lashes, but they had an entrancing curve of laughter in their luminous depths. They were animated, translucent mirrors of Siri's every emotion.

Cat, too, had been a whirlpool of emotions, but without the saving grace of lighthearted laughter. Indeed, her emotional antennae had been so hypersensitive that the everyday trivialities often assumed dramatic proportions. Charlotte could look back on a girlhood of soothing strained nerves, administering to sick headaches, and inducing a brilliant young sister to relax, to enjoy herself, and come away from 'that blessed piano' for an hour or so.

Her eyes came to rest on an early portrait of Catherine in evening dress. It held pride of place in Siri's bedroom. Such indestructible beauty ... destroyed! Charlotte remembered the day of the plane crash as if it were yesterday. The strident call of the telephone cutting across the small hours, the pricking of nerves, the premonition of disaster.

Catherine and Stephen had both been killed on what was to have been their first concert tour of the United States. And if the ten-year-old Siri had not been in the middle of school examinations she too would have had her short life snuffed out like a candle. Charlotte sighed, deeply introverted ... 'rage, rage, against the dying of the light!' One could rage, but one could never bring them back!

Siri looked up from her exertions. She was in the middle of some swinging exercises, her slender young body moving with the grace of a dancer.

'Why the great sigh, Lottie mine?'

Charlotte shrugged and started to pull out dresses. 'Nothing, darling. Remembrance of things past, I suppose.'

Siri glanced at the clothes on the bed. 'None of these, my love. I've a mind to look arty.'

Charlotte looked merely pained. The child could look impossibly exotic at times, given her head.

Siri smiled at her aunt's revealing expression. 'I don't imagine the great Damian St. Clair will be thrown by a fashion plate—or will he?' One delicate, winged eyebrow flew up in satiric amusement. 'They say he's not *unobservant* of women,' she stressed dryly.

Charlotte snorted. 'That's the understatement of the year! But you're hardly a woman yet, darling. A mere child of seventeen.'

Siri had heard of Damian St. Clair's off-stage successes. He was reported to be notoriously attractive to women and equally notorious for sidestepping the issue of marriage. Barely thirty with a smouldering,

7

dark and intensely male beauty, he was already riding a comet in the demanding field of conducting. One of Australia's most distinguished exports, he had returned home for a brief rest period before the promised brilliant season of concerts he was due to undertake in England and Europe.

Charlotte and Siri had seen his first TV interview. He spoke with the fascination and the complete lack of condescension of the truly great or potentially so. Added to that was his powerful personal magnetism, strikingly apparent even through the medium of the camera.

There was no wonder at all at his phenomenal impact on the lady viewers, for the interview triggered off a series of lavish society parties given on the offchance that he might show up. To his credit, he attended a few, however briefly, precipitating a minor earthquake among the would-be 'Dianas' of any age up to fifty.

His professional side was an entirely different matter. Exhausted, as he had every right to be, he still proposed giving a series of ten master classes to the cream of the country's aspiring young pianists. Siri had been nominated by the Professorial board at the Conservatorium, but the final audition was to be held by the great man himself.

Siri followed her own judgment as to her outfit. She dressed in a black, knife-pleated midi, with a white silk collar and cuffs and tiny gold buttons marching down the front. To that she added black patent leather boots, and tied her back with a bow in black velvet. Satisfied with her appearance, she went through to the kitchen.

Charlotte looked up with a start. 'Gracious, Siri, you look like a dandy of some sort. Don't ask me what period.'

'I thought I looked rather fetching myself.' Siri's mouth tilted upwards, highlighted by a small velvety black mole at the corner. She took the steaming cup of coffee her aunt handed her.

'What have you decided on, dear?' Charlotte judged it time to ask the question.

'Either the Mephisto Waltz or the Chopin Ballade. I'll decide at the last moment,' Siri announced grandly. 'I'm in gear for both of them. I like to dress the part. A painting by Delacroix . . . a Chopin . . . a George Sand!' She struck a languid attitude.

'Nervous?' Charlotte asked, feeling a seething mass of jitters herself.

'Not yet, anyway.' Siri put her cup down again. 'You know, Lottie, I don't think I'm a dedicated pianist at all. Not like Mummy. Remember how utterly other-worldly she used to get? So immersed and oblivious. I used to steal into the music room to hear her play and it wouldn't have made the slightest difference if I'd made my entrance on the back of an elephant. Even Father didn't make any impression. Do you suppose *that's* dedicated? I don't think I could ever be like that.'

Charlotte looked back at her keenly. What a funny little girl Siri had been, so assured and self-contained. And she had to be. Cat had loved her daughter dearly, but she had neither the time nor the patience to be a real mother to her small offspring. Instead, Charlotte had seen to that, even in those days. She had always been there. Siri had recognised and accepted her mother's temperamental withdrawals almost before they became apparent, turning to Charlotte for the hundred and one things she couldn't bother her mother with. Yes, Cat had been a strange one, but so beautiful and so gifted they had, all of them, forgiven her everything.

Siri was doubly blessed in inheriting her mother's beauty as well as her father's stability, his easy acceptance of life and living. Poor Stephen, he had thrown away a promising singing career to manage Catherine. Charlotte shrugged off her reverie, this preoccupation with the past. Though there were no more tears left in her, there wasn't a day of her life that she didn't think of her brilliant young sister who was destined never to grow old.

'Lottie darling, you're acting very strangely this morning!' Siri was regarding her aunt with anxious eyes.

'It's the rain, darling. It always affects me this way. Now, I'll drive you in.' She walked off smartly to collect their coats and brollies.

'Oh no, you won't. There's no need for you to go out in the rain.' Siri followed her aunt out into the hallway. They argued all the way out to the car!

Damian St. Clair finished off his not-too-scathing comments on the most recent candidate and rang the bell at his hand for the next budding hopeful. The door opened and closed softly.

'Serena Linton,' he read aloud without looking

up. His voice was like black velvet to match the rest of him, Siri thought, as she stood hesitating just inside the door, with every nerve on edge. She felt almost ill now, overawed by his aura of brilliance, the physical perfection she distrusted in a man.

'Come and sit down before you go to the piano,' he murmured in a low, preoccupied voice, noting something down on the paper.

Siri walked soundlesly over the wine-coloured carpet, amazed she could do even that.

'Now, Serena . . .' St. Clair broke off abruptly, but gave no other sign of his reaction to her unfurling beauty. His dark eyes, under their strongly marked brows, momentarily flashed. That was all. She rather evoked a camellia bud, a useful attribute for the concert platform. By all the laws of human compensation she should have no talent at all. She was hauntingly lovely, or at least she would be, as soon as she lost that curiously innocent girlishness. There was no onslaught of rich colouring, only the bone structure, the illumination of black and ivory and the shimmer of great smoky irises. He spoke again, rather harshly, a frown gathering.

'Serena,' he repeated. 'I don't know that it's appropriate!'

'Perhaps Siri, my aunt's version,' she offered, her voice faltering at his rather daunting expression. Surely it couldn't matter that much to him? Her voice was like honey and surprisingly mature for a girl of her age.

'Siri!' He repeated the name, slowly, consideringly, without comment. 'I couldn't possibly have seen you before, could I?' He regarded her through half-closed lids.

'My mother, perhaps,' she suggested. 'Catherine Frampton, the concert pianist. I'm said to resemble her.'

St. Clair swung up from the chair, very tall, very virile, emanating a powerful sexual radiance that even Siri, completely unawakened to the lure of the flesh, could hardly fail to recognise.

'Of course.' He turned back to her, his dark eyes explicit. 'Shall we see if you play just one half so well,' he drawled, rather sarcastically to Siri's sensitive ears. His dark head briefly indicated the Steinway and Siri went across and adjusted the seat. She was on her own now and she knew in her heart that she was not a quarter as good as her mother. Almost immediately a terrifying silence fell across the room, attacking her nerve centres and blurring her vision. Surely he could hear the painful thud of her heart? He stood with his back to her, impossibly demanding, critical to a fault. She could feel his antagonism. He was ready to pounce like a great black cat-man. Her fingers came down on the keys, but she had to sit quietly for a moment before the sickness passed.

The Chopin F Minor Ballade was one of her great favourites. It was dramatic and passionate, lyrical and rhapsodic, and demanded an impressive show of technique. St. Clair stopped his pacing after the brief introduction. The meltingly lovely slow waltz appeared and was repeated, then elaborately decorated. The nervous impetuosity of her start had given way to a deep lyricism and a crystalline purity of tone.

She had considerable style and an artistic insight unusual in her age group. His lean, arrogant face was intent on her performance. There were technical deficiencies apparent, probably due to her physical limitations. As it was she had considerable control of dynamics. The *tour de force* of the coda came to a close. Siri rested, her pallor very pronounced against the raven sheen of her hair.

He was beside her, the crisp efficiency of his tone jerking her back to reality.

'Show me your hands,' he ordered briefly.

She gave them up to him, then found herself starting at the shock of physical contact. Her eyes flew to his. He barely noticed her, his dark face remote, absorbed in some private thought. Her hands were very white and slender with long pointed fingers. They were beautiful hands, but the span was barely adequate for the demands of high virtuosity, he thought dispassionately. She could, of course, specialise and thus avoid certain technical hazards. He seemed not to notice that he still held her like a bird in the hand.

'You have a limited span, my child. I suppose you are aware of it?'

Siri nodded. 'I had thought of specialising, building up a suitable repertoire. Music is my life, though I don't aspire to the top rank.'

He dropped her hand as though it no longer interested him and turned back to the window. The weather was starting to clear and great patches of blue were making their welcome appearance. A brilliant silvery light lit up the camphor laurel.

'Have you ever thought of accompanying?' he asked in a cool, disinterested way. 'You might find the top rank there. You have sensitivity ... a most commendable singing tone.'

Siri looked crushed. She stared at his back, flushing unhappily. 'No, I haven't. And neither would I.' Her voice fell almost flat with her dashed hopes. 'I wouldn't care to share the limelight, you see.'

He turned to face her. His dark, sardonic face glimmered with amusement. He understood perfectly. He would never have consented to shared limelight himself. He narrowed his eyes after a few seconds' pause.

'Very well, Miss Linton. I will be including you in my master classes. It's no concession, so you needn't look so tragic. The next few years will make or break you.'

The note of dismissal in his voice was unmistakable. His attention seemed already elsewhere. Siri stood up. She was above average in height, but he was very much taller, making her tilt her head to him, only too conscious of his tremendous vitality and driving force.

'Thank you, Maestro,' she said with extreme courtesy. 'May I say I'm looking forward to them immensely?'

'They won't be plain sailing,' he warned her sardonically. 'So rid your mind of that. I'm a known slave-driver.'

She flushed a little under his scrutiny. He seemed to be looking right through her ... to the bone, seeking a flaw in her. He moved away from her to the door, holding it for the final entrant.

'Good day, Miss Linton.'

From the remote expression on his dark face it was impossible to say whether he would remember her at all, Siri thought, and hurried past him to the door. She was almost relieved to be free of his dark impersonality. There was a flicker of cruelty in the man!

Later Siri walked in the adjoining courtyard with her dearest friend, Jacqueline Winter. The intermittent bursts of sunshine seemed to soak the courtyard in peace and contentment. The outdoors always filled Siri with a sense of space and freedom. Now a radiant happiness seemed to be growing inside of her, warming, flaming, burning through her. She almost expected some comment from Jacky. Raindrops off the umbrella of the weeping elm fell on to her cheeks like petals. A shaft of sunlight slanted across the pathway, firing each quivering dewdrop.

Jacky, one whole year older and a budding mezzo-soprano of promise, was still talking. Siri had heard it all so many times before that she didn't have to listen at all. Jacky was passionately concerned with what she wrongly called her limited range and was dead set on hitting top A, today of all days. Her impassioned self-denouncements were to be taken with a huge grain of salt, Siri thought affectionately. Jacky was really very pleased with herself. Many had been the time when they had battled it out for the honour of soloist with the Conservatorium choir, with Jacky winning more often than not. But now Jacky wanted Siri's soprano secret of hitting top A.

'You *are* listening, Siri?' Jacky turned on her fiercely.

'Of course, my pet.'

'Be an angel and show me. Just once. You've got a very good voice for a pianist.'

Siri smiled at her. 'You're pushing it, Jacky, and well you know it. You're a mezzo, after all. The top notes aren't so very important at this stage.'

'Come on, stop the sermonising!' Jacky began to prod Siri's diaphragm. An interested sparrow flew all about them, then perched on the fat cupid in the centre of the sunken garden, turning his bright eyes on them and ruffling up his small breast feathers.

Siri laughed. 'My audience!' Glowing herself, with the air heavy with jonquils, she closed her eyes, turned her face to the sky, and then out of her streamed four consecutive top A's; round, floating, powerful and effortless.

'My stars!' Jacky fell to re-prodding Siri's diaphragm, her ribs, the small of her back. 'That was absolutely marvellous. But where did it come from?' If there was a way, she would find it. Jacky was a very headstrong girl, determined and ambitious. A window opened out above them. Damian St. Clair put his dark head through it and claimed their attention.

'Come up here, would you, Miss Linton! Right away, if you please.'

Jacky drew in a long gasping breath. 'Now you're for it! Yelling like that in the courtyard. The great man's offended.'

'To hell with the great man,' Siri said, equally fierce, although her face had whitened. She re-entered the building and walked up the flight of stairs. St. Clair was at the door. He beckoned her in without preamble.

'I've no time for preliminaries,' he said briefly. 'We'll go through the major scale by semitones. Sing the vowel that comes easiest—*Ah*, most likely.'

Siri had no time to be nervous. In fact, because no one really expected her to *sing* she followed his accompaniment freely and easily; a bright, clear soprano, her voice rounded and even through all registers.

'Sing something,' he ordered without even looking up.

'*Songs My Mother Taught Me*,' she suggested. 'I know that.' She leaned against the piano, puzzled by his interest. He played the introduction a tone higher than she was used to.

It wasn't possible a young girl should have that curious veil of sadness in her voice, he thought with complete objectivity; the potential to portray a limitless range of emotions. It was unbearably moving. He should have guessed from her speaking voice that she could sing. That peculiar vibration from the throat was always a sign. His hands fell away from the piano. But what could he do with her? She would have to be carefully handled. Castelli might be persuaded to take her on—certainly on his say-so.

He turned to her with a characteristically decisive

17

gesture. 'I think we've found your true métier. Nature has been lavish with her endowments. I wonder why?' A spasm of mockery crossed his face. 'You seem disappointed ... surprised,' he added, a shade irritably in the face of her silence.

'I am surprised,' Siri agreed quietly. 'Fair or unfair, I've never thought of being a *singer*. My whole mind has been set on becoming a *pianist*.'

He considered her gravely for a moment, then made a deliberate effort to speak as though his professional integrity demanded some comment. 'It's not as unusual as you seem to think,' he pointed out dryly. 'Some of our greatest vocal artists are gifted musicians. The one contributes to the other enormously. I would have expected you to appreciate the fact.' With his dark eyes on her Siri felt detached from reality. She could sense his baffling antagonism, yet those eyes were very hard to evade.

'You want to be famous, don't you?' he asked with mingled amusement and impatience.

'Of course, who doesn't?'

He smiled, which made a rather devastating transformation of his sardonic dark face. 'Quite a lot of people, actually. Not everyone has the head for crowning achievements. There *are* disadvantages, my child, but they don't weigh in the long run.'

She stood looking at him. How long had she known him? Two ... two and a half hours? It just didn't seem possible. None of it did.

'You live with your family?' he questioned her.

'My aunt, mother's sister, Charlotte Frampton.'

St. Clair got up from the piano. 'Leave me the

telephone number, like a good girl. I'll have to get in touch with her.'

Siri went to the desk and wrote the number down for him. He took the slip of paper, folding it in his lean strong hands. Quite without volition, Siri said the first thing that came into her head—something she was to curse herself for afterwards.

'How strange,' she murmured, her eyes on him. 'I've only known you two hours, yet I feel I've known you all my life. How do you account for it?' Her great smoky eyes were very young, very appealing.

His dark face loomed above her, its expression enigmatic. 'You're startlingly direct, aren't you, child? With your looks it's a dangerous quality.'

She turned away from him, flushing, feeling the rebuff in his words. There was some added complication she was vaguely aware of.

An ironical smile lit his face. 'The interview is at an end, Serena. You may tell your aunt I shall be in touch with her, this evening most probably. I have very little free time.'

Siri nodded her head briefly, feeling the hot colour in her cheeks subsiding. Wild horses couldn't have dragged from her another 'thank you, Maestro'. She walked to the door of her own accord. Damian St. Clair was an impossible man. Brilliant, yes, wonderful to look at, yes, but what a hard, uncaring man!

He rang that evening at seven-thirty. Siri went out purposely. Charlotte, forewarned, had stayed at

19

home to answer the phone. Briefly she regretted having to put off the weekly bridge party.

'Damian St. Clair here, Miss Frampton.'

His voice was beautiful and quite disturbing, Charlotte thought, susceptible to voices. But then so was Siri's utterly perplexing news.

'Yes, Mr. St. Clair,' she answered calmly, 'I was expecting your call.'

Amusement deepened his voice. 'I would like to speak to you in person, Miss Frampton, if we could arrange a mutually convenient time.'

Charlotte was nothing if not prompt. 'What about this evening? I've stayed home especially.'

He laughed, a far too attractive sound. 'Couldn't be better. Shall we say thirty minutes? It will take me that long to get there.'

Charlotte almost gasped. 'You have the address, then?'

'I have my methods, madam,' he answered with complete self-assurance, and rang off in her ear.

He was even more devastating in person. Charlotte showed him into the living room, vividly aware of his effect on women in general and her young niece in particular. He was quite extraordinarily attractive—too much so, she decided with unusual prejudice. She took his coat. He was wearing a black polonecked sweater and narrow black slacks. The outfit became him like no other. Well, really! Charlotte thought laconically as she turned back to him and caught the amused tug to his mouth.

'Something amusing you, Mr. St. Clair?'

The black eyes mocked her. 'Your attitude, madam. Very commendable, very protective. I can see you weighing me up with the eyes of an inexperienced seventeen-year-old and then as a mature woman. Am I right?'

Charlotte laughed, feeling the pull of the man. It was a pretty laugh and quite natural. 'How right you are! Please forgive me. Would you care for a drink? It's such a cold evening.'

Damian relaxed, his black eyes brilliant with amusement. 'At the risk of causing further concern, could you make it neat Scotch?'

'Most certainly I can. I fear you've stumbled across my fiercely aunty side. I do have others.' She walked over to the cabinet and took out the whisky decanter and two crystal tumblers.

Damian liked her. She had only a shadow of her sister's remembered beauty, but a look of warmth and distinction that was very attractive. The child was fortunate to have such an aunt. He accepted the glass and waited until Charlotte had taken a chair opposite him.

'Now what is all this about Siri?' Her eyes were very blue and direct.

Damian sat forward, his dark good looks intensified by the flickering flames of the fire. 'I think your niece has, rather I *know* she has, tremendous vocal potential. Surely you've noticed?'

He made that sound vaguely accusing. Charlotte frowned. 'Of course I have. Her father had an exceptional voice, but you must see that Siri has been training for years as a *pianist*. It was Catherine's

21

dearest wish.' She suddenly looked distressed.

'But Siri is not her mother.' St. Clair was adamant. 'I seem to remember Catherine Frampton as more in the heroic mould than her daughter, or am I mistaken?'

Charlotte looked up. 'Siri's much slighter, if that's what you mean.'

'Exactly, and Siri's hands correspondingly so. She is a highly gifted young woman, but she does have a limited span, as I told her. It would exclude a great deal of the virtuoso repertoire, you know. But that's not what interests me and I want to discuss with you. She has a truly beautiful voice, lyric in quality, great sensitivity, dramatic ability, and she will be in a year or so a ravishing beauty. There's a great future in opera for her. You must be prepared to take my word for it, and it should be sufficient. Our audiences demand far more than beautiful voices these days. Siri has everything to match—the voice, the face and the figure, an irresistible combination at the box office.'

His forcefulness hit Charlotte like a blow. 'You're very persuasive, Mr. St. Clair,' she said, her voice dragging. St. Clair swung up, suddenly irritated. He leant against the mantelpiece, his eyes leaping with some inexplicable emotion.

'My dear Miss Frampton, I'm not trying to be persuasive. I'm *telling* you something—something of importance. Your niece has it in her to be a great singer and you and I are going to see to it that she becomes one. Is that quite clear?'

'Oh, very much so.' Charlotte almost laughed.

She had seen too much of the artistic temperament to be offended by it; the high-handed air of command, and in her own living room!

'You know that I do,' she said calmly. 'How ridiculous we're being.' Her voice deepened. 'You seem more than ordinarily concerned with my niece, Mr. St. Clair. I don't think I'm mistaken.'

He looked down at her. At that moment his dark vitality had more than a dash of recklessness in it. Nevertheless, he spoke very dryly, precisely, matter-of-fact. 'I don't ordinarily go around talent-scouting, Miss Frampton. But in this case I think it worth my while. Shall we leave it that I'm vitally interested in putting my own country on the map, musically speaking?' His dark eyes rested rather ironically on her. 'I realise this intensive training will mean money—a lot of it, as it happens. I went through the same thing myself. But I'm prepared to back my own judgment ... financially. The burden will not fall on you. That aspect of it, of course, will be our mutual confidence. You have my word on it.'

Charlotte gazed into her glass unseeingly, then she lifted it and tossed off the contents. She found that she needed it.

St. Clair came back to sit beside her. 'It doesn't take much perception to realise that your niece is very dear to you, Miss Frampton.'

'Dearer than anything else in life,' Charlotte broke in with quiet insistence. 'When Siri first came to me I used to call her "my little treasure". I still think of her that way—my dear sister's child. Yet how happy this news would have made her father.

23

Stephen was a fine man, a fine singer. He abandoned his own career to manage Catherine's. Siri has inherited many of his shining qualities.' A tiny worried frown appeared between her eyebrows. 'But it's such a hard life, as you surely know, Mr. St. Clair. A kind of military existence, my sister used to say. I want so much for my little Siri. She could be anything, grace any scene. All the indications are there.'

Damian's eyes were hypnotic in their intensity. 'There are obstacles in every path, Miss Frampton. More, I know, in the way of the interpretive artist. Heartaches, disappointments, frustrations, the endless striving for the will-o'the-wisp perfection. But I believe Siri has got *it*. A star on her forehead.'

At his words, something inside Charlotte seemed to turn over. She loked around the room unseeingly. It glowed with colour, personal touches, a few fine paintings, which Siri and Charlotte had chosen together. How could she bear to lose her beloved niece. Ah well, wasn't the child bred to a musical career? Great talent carried great responsibilities with it. Her clear, trusting gaze came back to Damian's. His smile went straight to her heart, steadying her. There *was* another side to the man, an inherent tenderness, not often shown.

His voice was gently persuasive. 'You and I must see that Siri has a real chance at life, be properly equipped so that not a year of her precious youth is wasted. She must be ready by the time she's thirty. And by ready, I mean for international acclaim.'

At this Charlotte got to her feet, spring and elasticity in her step. 'I can see it's up to us to clear the way for *our* little Siri,' she stressed dryly.

'Exactly, Miss Frampton.' St. Clair looked across at her, his dark eyes alight with ironic admiration. 'And now shall we get down to detail?'

CHAPTER TWO

IT was five years before Damian St. Clair returned to Australia, and they had been five years in the headlines; five years of the long climb to the top. Secure now, at the summit, he had only to consolidate his position with the passing years.

His brilliance, his dedication, his impressive knowledge and authority, his ability to generate audience excitement, as well as an inborn theatrical flair, contributed in part to his extraordinary success. His name had acquired that ring heard only when speaking of 'star' quality.

Charlotte had word from him before the news was released to the Press. He had consented, in the face of more lucrative offers, to stage and conduct the coming season for the Australian National Opera Foundation, marking his triumphant return and the guest appearance of the German-born diva, Elisabeth von Richter, in the celebrated Ring cycle.

Charlotte waited for Siri to come home. She should be due any minute after a thirty-minute recording session with the National Broadcasting Commission. She heard the car come into the garage, then Siri's characteristic light and quick footsteps on the path. Charlotte walked out into the halfway to meet her.

Siri came into the pool of light as dark and beautiful as the star-studded night behind her.

'How did it go?' Charlotte noted the serious expression.

'Well enough. I wasn't entirely satisfied.'

Her aunt repressed a smile. Siri was nothing if not a perfectionist. They walked through to the kitchen for their nightly ritual of coffee and endless discussions.

'Clive play well?'

Siri's expression lightened. 'Like a dream. The perfect accompanist.'

'And what did he think of your performance?' Charlotte's voice was dry.

'Come on now, Lottie, you're having me on. You know as well as I do that poor old Clive just can't be objective as far as I'm concerned. I never believe a word he tells me.'

Charlotte laughed and filled the percolator.

'Legions of admirers and you've never so much as glanced at them! You make it too easy for me, Siri, truly you do. No late nights, no waiting up, no dire warnings, no earnest little chats. Siri, Siri, what is to become of me? I'm getting no practice at all as a young girl's adviser.'

'Perhaps it's all going to come at once, Lottie love, and then where will you be?'

Charlotte laughed, flicked on the switch, watching the red light come on. 'I have some news for you, darling.'

'St. Clair!' Siri said at once with uncanny perception. 'He's coming home.'

'My goodness, Siri!' Her aunt was genuinely

startled. 'How did you guess? It's all been very hush-hush!'

Siri's eyes glowed with amusement and some less definable emotion. 'The reverent tone, dear heart. You always adopt it when you speak of the great man. Well then, when does he arrive? Perhaps he'll condescend to explain why he never bothered to answer all the long letters he insisted I write to him.'

Charlotte was moved to protest. 'But, Siri dear, surely you haven't forgotten your pearls. They must have cost a fortune. I still can't think how I allowed you to keep them.'

Siri touched her long white throat without being aware of it. 'My pearls, yes! Out of all proportion to merely winning the Sun Aria, don't you think?'

Charlotte shook her head. They had worried her, those pearls! But St. Clair had been adamant. Siri was to have them. To keep them and that was that! Not just a short string either, Charlotte reflected a shade unhappily, but a lustrous length falling to the delicate curve of her breast.

Siri fixed her with a sardonic eye. 'Which reminds me, Lottie dear, you never have shown me any of his letters to *you*. I hope they've been quite proper. What on earth does he find to say? It's as well you hide them so successfully or I'd be tempted to find out.'

Charlotte looked at her niece keenly. She was inclined to believe her. Had Siri known it, the letters were all to do with her voice, or her training or some such thing. He had been most explicit with his instructions and he expected them to be carried out to

28

the letter. Such funds as were necessary were paid directly into Charlotte's bank.

'He'll be here in a fortnight, Siri. After that, the Season. I had word today.'

Siri was silent, a frown puckering her forehead, so Charlotte decided to change the subject. Her niece changed in some inexplicable way whenever they discussed St. Clair. She herself had grown used to thinking of him as Damian, but Siri, strangely enough, gave the impression of being vaguely antagonistic. Not at all what one might have expected.

'I've some other news, darling,' she said swiftly. 'I've found a new market in the States.'

'Why, Lottie, that's marvellous!' Siri put her cup down resoundingly. 'Which ones did they want?'

The two women fell into animated discussion. Charlotte was, and always had been, a talented commercial artist, but it wasn't until she came up with her 'Siri face' that the work and the money had started to pile in. Now Siri's childhood face, the enchanting little girl with enormous eyes, peered out of countless greeting cards. The face never varied, only the colouring and the hairstyle, the fascinating little costumes. The cards were endlessly popular and a great commercial success.

For that, Charlotte was everlastingly thankful. The one thing she had religiously kept from Siri was the fact that Damian St. Clair paid for every aspect of her training. Charlotte could never have managed it even with their combined resources, for Siri had a small private income from her mother. A white lie had been necessary. Siri's parents had left money in trust for their daughter to continue her musical training. Siri had accepted it without question. Of course, Siri did contribute with quite sizeable fees here and there as a professional pianist and accompanist, although her full-time vocal studies, combining stagecraft and acting, left little time for a more constant sideline.

It was almost midnight before they went to bed, a late night for both of them. Charlotte in her room heard the last brilliant cascade of sound, the glittering 'Sempre Libera' from *La Traviata*, the aria Siri had chosen for the National Finals. Then she heard Siri turn off her light. Charlotte did the same, smiling gently to herself. All the vocal gymnastics in the past had forced them into building their home on this high and rather difficult site. Now not even the trilling birds objected to this new intruder into their province. They still sang as madly, shouting together with such rapturous abandon that it was impossible to tell one from the other, and over the top of the ecstatic warbling came Siri, deeply committed to mordents and trills, arpeggios and rippling cadenzas.

Siri curled up in the window seat and looked out on the night. It was beautifully mild, with a wafer moon on high and a silver peppering of stars.

So he was coming back. She felt strung up, almost like crying. The thought of him had filled her days and nights for five long years. It had become an obsession, blocking her view of all others. Always in her heart and her mind she carried a picture of him, dark and powerful, gazing at her, through her, to the very core of her being. Not even his lack of response to the long student outpourings had dulled the brilliance of her memories of him. The night especially brought him back to her, compounded of the velvety darkness, the glitter of celestial fires, the emotional nocturnal romanticism ... At least she could be grateful to him for entrusting her training to Madame Castelli. They were now far more than teacher and pupil, but friends and colleagues.

Rosa Castelli, the once shining light of La Scala, was not only an exceptional teacher, but a woman of great intelligence and perception. Always guiding, never forcing, she judiciously carried the flag for technique until in the early days Siri had felt like screaming with the endless scales and exercises. But the results! The five years of association had reaped enormous rewards. Siri was an ideal student, throwing herself into her studies with insatiable yearning. Her control and flexibility bore testament to the long hours of practice and the 'Rosa Castelli' method.

The few people who heard Siri were impressed. Madame did not encourage public performance until such time as she judged advisable, allowing the voice and the technique the correct time for flowering. Then came the National Grand Opera Competition. Siri had been ready. She smiled in the darkness. The night of the finals! The one and only time she had ever seen Lottie go to pieces.

Her aunt had been a bundle of nerves, unable to sit in the auditorium but condemned to pacing the long corridors. Siri's hand found the delicate hollow at the base of her throat. Her pearls! How exquisite they were and, wonder of wonders, Lottie had let her keep them.

The night wind unfurled itself with a spreading of wings, beating through the dark rustling trees and shaking out the myriad scents of the garden. A cat in silhouette moved across the lawn with intimate knowledge of its blue-black domain.

Tonight there was an undercurrent of excitement in everything, a tingling awareness. It was as though destiny was pressing down on her. So he was coming back. Siri trembled with fear and fascination. Did he mean to take control of her future? The world narrowed to her view from the window, her own segment of the star-studded sky. Why was everything so different at night? Why did you succumb so easily to its mysterious influences—but there was a long day ahead of her.

Siri went back to bed and slipped under the covers. She lay quite still and tried to compose herself, but her mind kept racing onwards. She started breathing deeply, deeply, until the slow relaxation spread throughout her body with a delicious feeling of well-being until presently she drifted off to sleep.

In the morning the sun was shining from a cloudless sky and the wattle was out all over the hillside. Siri drove into the city armed with the score of *Rigoletto*. She was studying the part of Gilda, which Madame assured her no coloratura soprano could afford to be without. It was a pity, because she didn't care for it. The opera, yes—the part, no. Siri couldn't identify herself with the tender young maiden ascending the steps of her room, singing of her heart's first stirrings—the graceful 'Caro nome'. She preferred the blood and thunder of Tosca or Santuzza perhaps, but Madame thought otherwise. Siri waited outside the studio for Madame to open the double doors—the room was reasonably sound-proofed—promptly at ten. Not a minute either way was permitted.

Madame herself was inside, vocalising with an astonishing agility for a sixty-five-year-old. She broke off in mid-flight, then opened the door. Short and plump, she wore her touched-up hair arranged artfully on top of her head.

The black eyes snapped, 'Ah, Serena! *Mio Dio! Bella, bellissima, signorina!*' She approved her pupil from head to toe. 'Come in, come in, child, we waste time already.'

Siri followed the short imposing figure into the studio, which was a veritable Aladdin's cave, filled with gorgeous knick-knacks and paraphernalia, and a bower of greenery. On the glossy lid of the piano stood autographed photographs of the great ones, the illustrious stars of the past—Caruso, Chaliapin, Patti, Tetrazzini, Destinn, always scrupulously dusted in the same order. Siri wondered if it was personal preference.

Madame caught her train of thought. 'Ah, the past! How I long for it.' She clasped a hand to her full bosom. '*Stranziante!* So much of the best, and all gone from us. The ideas, the designs, the music, the melody, the life-blood of opera, our great and glorious Verdi. The beautiful, the balanced, the timeless.' She threw up a plump hand for the present.

'The audiences, Serena. Our audiences, they looked at us with one face. They adored us. But today, *grande cielo!* did you ever see such a hotchpotch, such an incredible cross-section as attend our concerts? No accounting for it, I tell you, for taste or for talent.'

Siri let her flow on. 'When I was young, *che fole!* I yearned for possessions, jewels, furs, beautiful clothes.' Her voice dropped a full octave. 'Of course I had lovers, but no acquisitions, without money, you see. How life teaches us. Now I am content, living near my son, my grandchildren, working with such a beautiful voice as your own.' Her tone altered perceptibly. 'He is returning. You know this.' Madame rolled her eyes with truly Latin vivacity. '*Un genio e molto simpatico*, that one.'

Siri fingered her score. 'It would seem so, Madame. The papers have it this morning.'

The black eyes were shrewdly assessing. 'So, we will surprise him. *Fate bene*, Serena. Your Gilda, where is it?'

Siri put the open score in front of her teacher.

CHAPTER THREE

IT was a matter of course that Siri received a gilt-edged invitation to the first lavish party given in honour of the visiting celebrities. Not only was she a young singer of promise, but a highly praised pianist and the daughter of the well-remembered Catherine Frampton. The Baroness von Richter, Signora Santegelo, and Damian St. Clair were to arrive Friday morning and the party was for the same evening.

Siri dressed with such extreme care that Charlotte was driven into calling it 'just plain finicky.' It took a complete change of dress before Siri was satisfied. It was absolutely imperative that she should look her best—no need to ask why, so Charlotte tactfully didn't. All Charlotte did do was stand by and help her niece out of the silver grey satin, which was quite beautiful, and into the stark simplicity of pitch black velvet. At least, Charlotte considered, Siri would be warm, for it was decidedly chilly outside.

But when Siri was ready Charlotte had to admit that her niece knew best. Black was her forte, enhancing the ivory smoothness of her face, neck and shoulders. The gown had a look of the medieval with its deep decolletage, long tight sleeves and flowing skirt. The pearls couldn't have had a more perfect showcase resting between the curves of her breast.

Siri flickered a light spray over the raven coils arranged at the back of her head. The front hair was drawn severely off her brow with only two curving tendrils brought forward in front of her small, close-set ears.

She turned to Charlotte, who was openly admiring. 'May I wear Mummy's earrings?'

'Of course, darling. Need you ask?'

Charlotte hurried away to get them from her small wall safe. Catherine had left several valuable pieces, necessary to her stage appearance, and Charlotte had held on to them through thick and thin. She took out the earrings and Catherine's engagement ring from which they had been copied, all lustrous pearls surrounded by the same sunburst of diamonds. The tears stood in her eyes, then she blinked them back fiercely lest Siri notice and be upset. She could look at nothing of her sister's without the tears starting.

Charlotte went back into the bedroom. 'Here you are, darling, and the ring as well, just for this evening. You look quite extraordinarily romantic. Something out of Tolstoy, in fact.'

She subjected her niece to the final scrutiny. Not a hair was out of place. Those great shining coils were a masterpiece, secured with invisible pins, seeming to draw back Siri's head with the weight of them. The door bell sounded.

'That's Clive now. I'll go and let him in.'

Charlotte went out to the hallway. There was never any delay with these young musicians. Punctuality had been drilled into them from childhood.

Siri was close behind her, adjusting her black velvet stole embossed with silver and gold medallions.

Clive looked his enslavement. He was hopelessly in love with Siri, but mercifully not violent about it. That would have been too much. As it was, he was content to worship from afar. Charlotte approved, but could not understand it ...

The party was at the home of society's leading light, Mrs. Vivian Visconti, born Vera Hull, which evolved into the more phonetically pleasing Vera Hill when she was about the age of eighteen and finally settled on Vivian Visconti, some said for purely euphonious reasons. It was quite untrue. Hugo Visconti had made his first million by the time he was forty. He was now ten years richer.

Their home was superbly pseudo-palazzo, on a terraced hillside overlooking the harbour. The entrance was through a formal garden in the Italian manner which led to the inevitable swimming pool with its own charming pavilion built round it, and thence to the house proper.

The mood of the Roman Villa was set. The hall was decorated in the grand manner with two life-size classical figures, both female. The figures, in fact, had once been male and female, but had proved too much of a talking point, while the trompe d'oeil wallpaper of shuttered windows together with various Mediterranean pieces completed the picture.

The large, beautifully proportioned living room

was a decorator's dream, the entire background ranging from blanc-de-chine porcelain to ivory walls and the thickly-piled vanilla beige carpet. The one brilliant accent was crimson, which was boldly stated in the silk-lined niches housing precious objets d'art on either side of the truly magnificent fireplace, with its gilt-edged Venetian mirror.

An opera of voices all pitched a tone higher than normal emerged from the room. It was blooming with lights and with flowers. Mrs. Visconti, or Madame Visconti, if you seriously wished to please her, was a violently affected woman whose bubbling effervescence could be converted into an impressive hauteur at a minute's notice. She greeted Siri and Clive with charming condescension, an impersonal hand on each arm, then drew them into the perfumed, bejewelled and highly stylish gathering.

Two well-known musicians were inside the ivory drapes in the middle of a prolonged and tumultuous argument about 'flu injections. They broke off to stare after Siri as though her beauty disturbed them immensely.

Through the open French windows leading on to the terrace was the double reflection of the moon. It had risen higher in the heavens while still floating over the harbour. Great splashes of colour, which turned out to be azaleas in copper tubs, gleamed in the half-light and couples like moths came and went from the champagne to the stars.

Siri found herself taken up by Jon Lawnton, the TV personality and compère of a weekly talent showcase with a high national rating. He was fair, quite attractive, but a lot smaller than one would have imagined. He sat a lot higher when in front of the cameras. He did have enormous personality and an equal amount of cheek, Siri decided. He had taken her face between his hands as if to feel the lovely shape of it.

'Exquisite, Miss Linton,' he murmured abstractedly. 'I may call you Serena? The bones of enduring beauty! I could use you on camera.' He took her arm with a leisurely movement. 'Come away with me, Natasha, out of this turbulent throng.' He steered her over to a quiet corner. 'Now tell me what you've been doing since the last time we met.'

Siri took his determined bonhomie in her stride, alive to the chatter around her. Groups were forming, dissolving, re-forming, swelling with new arrivals. Introductions were made to be instantly forgotten and enthusiastic greetings exchanged between who on earth was it? And always and all over there were sharp, confident faces keeping an eye on the door.

The celebrities arrived shortly before nine, Baroness von Richter, handsome and voluptuous, with the rarest kind of tawny colouring and the creamy skin of a blonde; and Signora Santegelo, a vibrant and voluble brunette, inches shorter but of equal plentitude. Siri scarcely noticed them. Her glance was caught and held by the dark attraction of his profile. He was standing quite still surveying the room with a calm arrogance, drawing every eye without the slightest conscious effort. The Baroness turned her splendid head encircled with braids and tossed off a remark to him. He looked down at her and laughed, his face bright and handsome. The smile was dazzling, disarmingly so, as she remembered.

'Handsome devil, isn't he? Such an air of command. They tell me he's got a violent temper, though. White-hot!' Lawnton breathed in her ear. 'I wonder if I could induce him to lose it on one of my programmes.'

Siri scarcely heard him. Her heart was hammering overtime.

'Ding, dong, dell, pussy's in the well.' He had noticed her abstractions. 'They all go round the bend, you know,' he added with absolute certainty.

Siri stirred. 'The only ones to do so to my knowledge have all been on trams.'

He laughed uproariously. Their hostess too was being astonishingly vivacious, assuming a thick Milanese accent in empathy with Santegelo. They were both in earnest conversation, neither comprehending, not as if it mattered anyway.

St. Clair moved further into the room with a lean and powerful grace. Siri's hand at her side clenched and unclenched. St. Clair was immediately swept up by his hostess.

'Maestro, I have so many people just dying to meet you.' She put a hand on his arm, leading him away with brutal determination.

'She'll trot beside him all night, mark my words,' Lawnton said maliciously.

'Rather sweet, that,' Siri remarked tonelessly.

'You sound a bit flat, love. Feeling the strain of

40

the social vortex?' He narrowed his eyes at her.

'Of course not. I'm more in the mood for fire-works.'

For a moment he looked highly diverted. 'Is that so! And you *sing* too. Quite divinely, as I recall. Wait until the gay throng melts a little, Natasha, my little Tolstoyan heroine.' His light eyes glittered with some sort of mischief. 'You haven't a motto by any chance?' he asked flippantly.

'Aim high,' Siri said promptly. 'And if you won't race away I'll tell you the story of my life.'

He laughed. 'Delighted, pet, but give me a minute to circulate.' Siri watched him take off in an un-deviating line to his hostess. It was shortly before first supper, after midnight, that Siri discovered the reason for his air of devilment.

'Ah, Miss Linton!' The Visconti advanced on her. 'I've been told you're going to sing for us.'

Siri saw through her golden mist. It must have been the champagne, she thought. Apart from that one brief moment she had only seen the back of St. Clair's handsome dark head, usually bent to the Baroness.

'My God!' Siri said two or three times to herself. 'Mr. Lawnton's little joke,' she explained out loud to her hostess.

'Come now, you've nothing to be ashamed of,' the Visconti murmured with no apparent connection. 'Shall we say in five minutes?' She turned away, obviously not expecting any opposition.

Siri met Jon Lawnton's eyes across the room. He

looked back unflinchingly, then raised his glass to her.

And this is where little Miss Linton comes to a very sad end, or the first discordant note in the gay little party, Siri thought, her mind clearing rapidly.

Von Richter was a dramatic soprano of unsurpassed power and polish, but she was not famous for her warmth or intensity, while Santegelo was an excellent navigator in the vocal stratosphere with an unremarkable middle register. That left her with what?

Santuzza, of course. The tragic Santuzza, that Eleanora Duse had brought to the stage with a passion no opera singer had ever surpassed. Mascagni had taken the story for his *Cavalleria Rusticana* an opera of passion, betrayal and swift retribution. The hot blood of the story coursed through the music with its fiery onrush of passions. The heroine, Santuzza, tells the story of her betrayal to Lucia, the mother of her lover. Siri felt herself into the role. It was easy, for not one word had to be spoken to her. Not one word, not one glance, and it would have been so easy! So gracious of the master. He had only to detach himself from the great tawny Baroness. She would soon run to fat if she wasn't careful, Siri thought on an unaccustomed wave of waspishness.

Madame Visconti introduced her to the sea of white faces. They looked up expectantly. 'Ladies and gentlemen, a moment, if you please.' She rapped on the piano. 'Later on in the evening we are hoping to be honoured by our beautiful and distinguished guests . . .' she bestowed an all-enveloping smile on

the divas, 'but now, one of our own young artists—
Miss Serena Linton. Many of you will remember
her mother, the beautiful and gifted Catherine
Frampton—' Well, she hoped they remembered, for
she certainly didn't herself!

There was a ripple of interest, a spate of gossip,
then the fateful introduction from the piano. Siri
settled into the loving curve of the Bechstein. Her
beauty silenced them and her detachment. She was
now completely outside herself, the rarest of flowers,
the singing actress.

'*Voi lo sapete, Mamma.*' The impassioned voice
spilled into the silence, rounded, sensuous, vibrant
with vocal colour.

Von Richter's head came up with the precise and
practical objectivity of her race. Santegelo's went
down. She looked as if she was hearing voices, nasty
voices. The heartrending outbursts of grief flooded
over them. '*Ah! l'amai*—I loved him!' The supreme
climax came on a brilliant top note. Siri's eyes found
St. Clair's—unwillingly, hypnotically. She was singing *to* him, *for* him. Yet he had no ears for it, for he
turned his head, averting his dark profile, a cold
remote head on a medallion.

There was complete silence for a few seconds,
then wildly appreciative applause—doubly dear,
because many of those present were hard-core pro-
fessionals, merciless in their judgements.

The applause continued. The conscious artist had
emerged, sure of herself and her gifts. Siri declined
to sing an encore, but moved away from the piano,
with Clive in attendance. A very white-faced Clive,

although he had accompanied her beautifully.

Later on in the evening when the Baroness had sung her Wagner and Santegelo her Rossini, there were many who thought the first performance of the evening had not been bettered, but had the wisdom to confine their opinions to the privacy of their own homes.

Siri was not there to hear either soprano. Clive felt a violent migraine coming on. Not the convenient, excuse kind, although he wasn't enjoying the party, but a humdinger with visual disturbances and accompanying nausea. Siri took charge, detaining her hostess for a minute—she wasn't allowed more—then hurrying her friend out to the car. Many times in the past Clive had come to her aid without thought of his own enjoyment. Besides, she hadn't enjoyed the party either. In fact she felt bitterly rejected. Put in her place where she firmly belonged . . . just another aspiring young singer.

Siri drove. 'Put your head back, Clive. I'll wind the window down a little. Some air might help.' She leaned across him.

'I'm sorry, Siri dear. I've spoilt your evening. You look so magical too. There was no one there to touch you.' He put a hand to the side of his head, groaning.

'Hush! Don't talk. I'll have you home in fifteen minutes.'

Clive's mother was waiting for him—a quite usual occurrence, although there was really no need. Mrs. Martyn was a widow and Clive was her only child, but she would dearly have liked Serena Linton for a daughter-in-law. Serena could help Clive with his music, be no end of help to him. She gave Siri a pale smile. 'You'll come in, dear. I have some hot Milo waiting.'

'Not tonight, thank you, Mrs. Martyn. Clive needs you. These headaches are becoming more frequent, aren't they?'

The older woman frowned. 'They are indeed, and his pills don't help much. Overwork, I expect. He doesn't put his feet up enough.' She flicked the switch for the old gas lamp converted to electricity that stood at the bottom of the garden. 'I'll leave this on for you, dear. Clive will pick up the car when he's able. Don't you go to the bother of running it back.'

Siri smiled. 'No trouble. I'll say good night, then.'

They both stood on the porch waiting until Siri started the car and drove away.

Siri, driving home, had only one thought in mind —to die of humiliation. A spasm of pain creased her forehead, so sudden and sharp that she made a small involuntary gasp aloud. After five long years of slavery and soul-searching ... *this*! She had been scorned and rejected. A woman of no importance!

CHAPTER FOUR

SIRI dreamed away the afternoon. She lay on her back in the thickly-piled grass, doing absolutely nothing. Now and again she looked up at the wattle tree with dreamy appraisal, seeing the silvery grey leaves with chinks of blue in between and the frail constellations making their first gauzy appearance. The same yellow gold was repeated all over the hillside.

On the grass beside her lay an unopened manuscript. Siri clasped her arms above her head, listening to the gentle swish of the breeze through the coral tree. Heavy pruning over the years had given it a weirdly attractive formation. One of her diminutive friends was in its top branches, pouring out a cascade of song that filled the air with a miracle of loveliness. Such a tiny frame to send out such a volume! It carried all over the hillside. Just as suddenly as it had begun, the song was abandoned.

Today the blue sky was dappled with fleecy white clouds, and the sun, ringed with a white-hot radiance, streamed down with a comforting flame that lured you into the very heart of existence. Siri blinked and shut her eyes for a moment. The silvery light through the foliage was dazzling.

Irresistibly her mind went back on the party and she knew a sensitive shrinking. Her vague emotions focussed into sharpest anxiety. She was doing herself violence, thinking of Damian St. Clair. Small isolated sounds came from the garden beyond her. She sighed deeply, stretching her arms in graceful abandon. A shadow fell across her. She gazed up transfixed, her mouth slightly parted with suspended breath. His tall figure loomed above her, his dark eyes directed upon her. The shock of it was beyond what she had power or will to withstand. The walls of the world contracted; they might have been alone in it for all Siri cared. Agitation swept over her, the need for self-protection. She brought up her hands and covered her face with the gesture of a ten-year-old.

'You foolish child!' He spoke without emphasis, deceptively gentle. Siri felt him lower his long length to the ground beside her. He took charge of her fluttering hands with merciless efficiency, drawing them away from her face. 'And how discourteous you are, Siri. After five long years of girlish outpourings you might at least tell me why you disappeared on the stroke of midnight. Surely that pale streak of misery wasn't your Prince Charming?'

Siri drew in her breath, softly, guardedly, her great smoky eyes enigmatic.

His voice was edged with delicate mockery: 'So silent, Serena, with all the lovely tales we've ever heard or read!' His hand came out to tap her cheek. It was cool, but the coolness was only a pretence, for warm blood flowed beneath his hand, staining the ivory pallor.

She wanted to cry out: 'Please don't hurt me.

47

You can, so easily!' But she could manage nothing at all.

He made a small, mocking noise. 'That look of innocence is still there. Even your temples are touched with a kind of helpless fragility. It's rather depressing after all this time. I don't know quite what I expected.'

Siri lay helpless under his gaze. Life was such an infernal thing. You couldn't alter it by one little inch, she thought fatalistically.

'What are you thinking about, Siri?' he asked with amused impatience. 'Or is it a secret?'

'Not at all,' she said bluntly. 'I'm thinking about you.'

His dark eyes glittered. 'Should it give you that wild rose colour?'

'Yes,' she said simply. 'Why did you never answer any of those girlish outpourings?'

His mouth twitched slightly. 'They were very sweet, Serena, but I never write letters. I'm in a very demanding profession. You could have made allowances for me.'

Her mouth quivered uncontrollably. She could slap him for his arrogance, the taunting note in his voice. 'Yes, of course,' she said dispiritedly.

'Then why look so desperate, child? I was sure you would appreciate my position.'

'Yes, Charlotte did too,' she murmured dryly. Charlotte had been the recipient of innumerable letters, but he didn't condescend to answer *her*. Beneath the silken lids her eyes were alive with restlessnes and an unbearable kind of anger. He was

48

making a fool of her, shattering her hard-won veneer of composure.

His brief laugh came to her, disciplined, faultless. 'What a romantic child you are, Siri! A case of arrested development.'

Her eyes flew open wrathfully with a quick change of temper. Her stormy glance rested on the sensuous mouth above her. It blatantly mocked her. *And for this she had waited and waited and waited.* She came to her feet with the grace of a Pavlova. 'What were you expecting in five short years? "A Thousand and One Nights" to be written all over me?'

He was beside her, drawling sardonically, 'And why not? A little experience never hurt anyone. Even you, Scheherazade. In fact, in your case it's a basic essential.'

She caught in a shuddering breath, but his mouth was upon her, insistent, wildly insistent, forcing her over the threshold of innocence and into the fevered world of the senses. Her taut immobility changed to a frightening surrender. He drew her still closer, careless of hurting her, for her response was a woman's, not the smoky-eyed child he had thought her.

What shall I do? How shall I escape from this? Siri thought desperately. His mouth and his arms, his hard body were against her. The touch of him, the male scent of him, shot through her like a mighty tornado. Her brain threw out messages—the need to withold from him, but her senses were hopelessly committed.

Blindly she spoke against that hard, punishing mouth. 'Please, don't! No more, I can't bear it.'

His arms fell away from her, leaving her swaying unsteadily like an exhausted flame. There was a fine-drawn tension in his face. 'That was a much-needed lesson for both of us and one I don't care to repeat.'

'You're ruthless, aren't you?' she said slowly, fighting for breath. 'You're cruel and you're ruthless, and I never realised it before. You're out to hammer home every little point, and in this case you've succeeded. I'm a green girl no longer, and I don't thank you for it!'

Her anger and tension was everywhere—in the air, in the flickering green shadows, in the unwonted pallor of her skin and the deepening lustre of her hair. Tears swam across the dark image of his face. One braid had loosened, falling in an inky curtain, rain-straight.

Slowly he reached out and tucked the thick swathe behind her ear, his own anger tempered by her picturesque dishevelment.

'Experience inevitably means more pain than pleasure, my poor Serena, but I take back all I said about wide-eyed innocence. You'd never have been able to kiss like that.'

The effrontery of it almost took her breath away. Her face flamed under his eyes. 'If you'd more experience in musical comedy than grand opera, Maestro, you'd know kissing comes naturally!'

He laughed, a brittle sound, without humour. 'Does it indeed, Serena? I've never know anyone as remotely proficient even after years of practice.'

There was a flicker of pain on her white brow. 'I'm absolutely right about you, aren't I? You're conceited beyond repair, ruined by adulation.' She brushed grass seeds off her slacks, hiding her face from him.

'Forgive me, Serena.' He bowed ironically. 'But you've as much knowledge of men as a doe has of tigers in the jungle.'

Her eyes flashed to his face. 'Thank you, but your opinion of me, whether flattering or not, proves that you have a certain interest in me. My voice, of course.'

His hands closed over the fine bones of her shoulders. 'Such intuitive intelligence! Yes, Serena, you moody child, you do *sing* rather well. The five years haven't entirely been wasted at any rate.'

She looked at him with hesitant reproach, but he only smiled. His eyes were full of a taunting diablerie that made his face especially vivid. She moved away from him, pushing back her disordered hair. She felt very young and uncertain beneath her pose of female condescension.

His eyes narrowed on her haughty young profile. 'How long do you propose to keep *that* up? It's not the real thing, you know.' He glanced back to the house, where a car had just pulled into the driveway. 'That's your aunt returning, unless I'm very much mistaken. Let's go up, there are quite a few things I have to discuss with her.' He took her hand and pulled her back up the hill, his manner purely tyrannical.

So this was to be the way of it, Siri thought wretchedly. She glanced up at his profile, at this dark invader who was taking her compliance with his every wish so very much for granted. She trembled convulsively and walked beside him, head up and silent, with the clear winter sunshine bright around them.

Charlotte gave him a glowing welcome. Siri was surprised. Her aunt was a warm and loyal friend, but she was slow to give her allegiance. Not, apparently, in this case. They must have been marvellous pen-friends, Siri considered cynically. She watched them in easy conversation, their faces alight with mutual interest. Such a ripple of defiance rushed through her that she executed a chain of pirouettes out into the kitchen to one of Lucia di Lammermoor's brilliant phrases of vocalisation.

It didn't take him long to catch up with her! 'What in sweet hell was all *that* about?'

Her head drooped like a sad child's, but her chin was stubborn.

He leaned against the door jamb, casual and relaxed, but his voice was edged with sarcasm. 'Fluency and flexibility are only two of the requirements of Lucia, my dear Miss Linton. However brilliant the soprano, she must still convey the mental state, the sense of the sad fate of the heroine. *That* was pure bravado!'

'True, too true.' She adopted his own satirical tone, not even remotely matching it in quality. 'You know, you look uncommonly like Damian St.

Clair, the eminent conductor. You have the same *unfrivolous* face. It's a wonder I dare approach you.'

He came away from the door with lithe purpose. 'Yes, isn't it, but the fun's over. Come along and show me what you've been up to. I have an hour to spare you.' He took hold of her wrist, gone limp, steering her through to the music room. Charlotte had the presence of mind to be there before them. Now order reigned. Siri usually left her scores and piano music all over the place, in harmonious pandemonium. Charlotte had the feeling that St. Clair wouldn't appreciate it.

His dark eyes swept the room before he sat down at the piano, the transformation from mere mortal to eminent conductor astonishingly complete. He was now wholly intent on Serena Linton—singer. His dark eyes were alive with a brilliance that denied everything but work, work, work!

Siri was a little slower to adjust, even bemused by his professionalism. She made an attempt to compose herself.

'Whenever you're ready, Miss Linton,' he drawled in the voice of a complete stranger. Nevertheless it had the power to bring her to complete attention. 'What roles have you off?' he asked, crisply authoritative.

'Lucia, Violetta, Leonora, Rosina, Tosca, Aida. I love Aida.' She almost rattled them off in nervous haste.

'Norma?' he asked with a quick lift of the head.

'I'm studying it.' Siri visibly swallowed.

'You haven't mentioned Gilda.'

'Oh, Gilda!' She blithely dismissed poor demented Gilda. 'I don't care for Gilda at all. It's not *me*.'

'Really!' The black eyes snapped sardonically, the inflection in his voice brought a flush to her cheeks. 'Do you think you could bear to sing me something that is *you*?'

His extreme sarcasm was not lost on her. She turned very quickly and ruffled the sheets of music turning up *"Aida"*— 'Ritorna Vincitor!' She placed it in front of him on the music stand.

He rounded on her at once, his dark face rather cruel in its condemnation. 'My darling child! I'm well aware of your *passionate* nature. It's your technique I'm interested in. Kindly pass me something else, before I lose all patience. The despised Gilda will do.'

Siri sighed loudly, bringing instant censure on her head. He stood up in a fury, shaking her hard. 'Look at me when I speak to you. That's better. Now, once and for always, when we're working together, I want complete professionalism. And that entails no antics, no feminine exhibitions, no tears and no tantrums. I want your entire attention directed on me and your score. Is that clearly understood? It's the only way I find acceptable.'

Her grey eyes held his until she could stand it no more. Her eyes dropped, dazzled with the tears he despised. All thought of levity had now left her. She turned away and found 'Caro Nome'.

It was a tempestuous hour. Siri, lulled by Madame Castelli's infrequent but fervent compliments, was incited to near-rage by his all-out attack on her interpretive powers. Not a word, not a phrase was in order.

'Serena?' He looked sharply at her. She had her head turned away from him, blinking back the sparking tears of mortification. 'You're being very adolescent, you know. It's hardly worthy of a performer, and more important still, you're wasting my time.'

She didn't answer but stood there silently, her profile outlined against the rose glow of the lamp.

'I'm merciless, you know.' The inflection in his voice was devastating. 'Quite merciless. Have you only just found that out?'

'Oh no, not at all. I found that out five years ago, Maestro. But I don't need your mercy!' Her high-cheekboned face was flashing with intensity.

He put a finger to her chin, bringing it round with a hard, imperative gesture. 'Have you gone out of your mind? Don't shout at me, my girl. You'll behave yourself in future, or remain a nothing. If you're going to come apart at the first sign of criticism you'll never make an opera singer. Not ever. Not in one hundred years of expert tuition.'

'Criticism!' Her voice broke like a child's. 'Artistic prejudice, I call it! You're rejecting my personality out of hand, totally rejecting it with your superior benevolence. A genius talking to a rather bright child. I am what I am, not as I exist in your imagination. I will not be made over in your image. Damian St. Clair, our brilliant concert pianist turned conductor! No, not at all. I have great drama myself, you know.'

He made no effort to control his anger, though he approved her healthy conceit. Conceit was indispensable to the highly vulnerable prima donna. It was the magic elixir to instil confidence, often in the face of inevitable and sometimes ill-tempered criticisms, but his demeanour was intimidating, making her regret her rash temper.

'You will *be*, Serena,' he said through clenched teeth, 'exactly what *I* want you to be. Allow me to know better than a precocious and opinionated student. I am telling you, and you will have the good sense to listen, that your conception of Gilda is totally wrong. Too much tension, too much of your precious drama.' His voice was unbearably cutting, the voice that had reduced many a big name to tears. 'I appreciate your considerable assets in that direction, my dear, but they are *not* required for this particular role. I gave your intelligence more credit than was due to it. You possess a naturally beautiful voice—what I require of you now is to place it at the service of a character penetration. In this case, poor maligned Gilda, who obviously doesn't appeal to you. I simply can't bear to have the part *yelled* at me.'

Her great eyes flashed at this final outrage and he carefully moved a vase from harm's way. 'No, don't interrupt, Serena, you're the kind of female who throws things. Now ....' He turned back to her and held her face with hard, hurting fingers, his eyes resting on her passionate, quivering mouth. 'Why so mutinous? I find it boring. You have an incredibly feminine aura, Miss Linton. Do try and use it to the right effect!'

Siri didn't answer but stood there, fighting back burning, hot tears. Those tears could wait until later. He was a fiend incarnate. And she had worked so hard! The endless hours of study, vocalisation—and all for nothing!

He made a sound of complete exasperation. 'Really, Siri, do you have to look quite so desperate? As though the world had come to an end. Will you never grow up?'

Her eyes continued to shimmer, but no tears fell. She had an iron control on herself. 'From this moment, Maestro,' she vowed in a fiery undertone.

He was completely unimpressed. 'Good,' he said off-handedly. 'In your case a little suffering is downright necessary.' Around the corners of his mouth there was an expression of amused tolerance. 'Now, shall we try it once more?'

He sat down at the piano and Siri began the aria, a sense of the inescapable settling on her. Her antagonism collapsed. He would always dominate her!

Her voice had a uniqueness, a sweet and secret sound that would become her most treasured possession. The fire had gone out of her, leaving her with the gentle submissiveness, the tremulous uncertainty of a young girl. She sang her Gilda with a vocal colour unlimited in its spontaneous purity. The extreme top note came out with entire certainty.

His hands dropped from the keys. 'Better!' he commented briefly. 'Given the right direction, you're capable of anything. You have the potential of an absolute soprano able to sing any role. But I'm not sure if that's wise. We shall see.' He moved swiftly. His mood had changed. He was a complete stranger again.

Siri started like a sleepwalker. 'It's quite simple then, isn't it? You'll grant me two or three hours a week and we'll meet, two dedicated musicians, with no thought in their heads but their work.' She looked enchantingly young and desperate.

His expression was a curious mixture of hauteur and amusement. 'You stagger me, child! What more do you feel yourself entitled to, I wonder?' His voice had a deceptive gentleness, but the line of his brows gave him a dangerous look.

Siri's eyes fell ... defeated.

Charlotte appeared at the door, a smile on her face. 'You will honour our humble abode for dinner, Maestro?' she asked with humour.

He gave her a brief, wholly charming smile. 'I'd like to, Charlotte, but I have an engagement I must honour.'

'Another time, then,' Charlotte said easily. The strain of the past hour was telling on Siri. She looked very white and exhausted.

'Ho-jo-to-ho?' Siri raised her eyes to him, her voice bitter-sweet.

His dark eyes glittered. 'I didn't say so, Serena. But while we're on the subject, be at the theatre Monday morning. The Baroness will be rehearsing *Walküre* then. You can hear her famous battle cry for yourself. She has a magnificent stage presence.

58

You'll learn a great deal from her.'

'A fit daughter of the Gods!' Siri seemed unable to control her runaway tongue. 'It's a wonder Wagner himself doesn't rise from the grave to applaud those top C's. I have all her recordings. All yours too, Maestro. Tell me, do you expect her to behave in a thoroughly warlike fashion this evening, or will she leave her spear at home?'

Charlotte looked from one to the other in astonishment. Siri seemed decidedly overwrought. The atmosphere fairly crackled with tension. St. Clair looked down at the pale face at his shoulder.

'You don't really expect me to answer that schoolgirl thrust, do you, Siri? You're not up to my mettle at all. Now, Charlotte, may I have a moment, outside? Adults only.' He flickered a brief, repressive glance at Siri and took Charlotte's arm, leading her out to the car.

When, later, Charlotte returned, she commented laconically: 'That was rather stormy, wasn't it, darling? I couldn't help overhearing. I do hope you'll be able to work together. It's such a great honour for you. You really mustn't try to antagonise him. He's not a man to stand for it—at all!'

'Oh, isn't he!' Siri jumped up, nearly capsizing her chair. 'Well, let me tell you, there's nothing I like better. He's insufferable, arrogant as the devil ... the be-all and end-all of creation. The demon Damian St. Clair!'

Charlotte showed not a spark of reaction. She smiled into her niece's great stormy eyes. 'Well, just see you make it to the theatre on Monday.'

'I'll be all respectful attention,' Siri said, sub-siding all of a sudden, feeling the calming effect of Charlotte's presence. 'Little girls should be seen and not heard, according to the great St. Clair.'

Charlotte's fine blue eyes were sparkling with amused appreciation. 'So you strike sparks off one another, do you? In a way it's only to be expected.'

Siri sniffed, defending herself hotly. 'At least, I'm open to suggestion. I'm not completely intolerant. *He's* the absolute limit!'

CHAPTER FIVE

THE curtain was rising on Act II of *Die Walküre* when Siri slipped into the darkened stalls of the theatre. Damian's dark head was outlined against the footlights, his whole being radiating power and authority. The orchestra swept into the Vorspiel, wonderfully descriptive, vibrant with elemental power, until with tremendous force on the trumpets and trombones the curtain rose on the wild mountain pass with its sloping gorge.

In the foreground stood Wotan, the chief of the Gods, in a jade pullover of all things, and Brunnhilde, his favourite daughter, in a superb St. Laurent ensemble, in which she had no hope of bridling her steed for battle. But her weirdly wonderful battle cry taking in the not too often heard top C's was hurled forth in a clean thrust of joyous ease and abandon.

Ho-jo-to-ho heiaha! The words rattled the empty stalls and sailed into the gods, the cry of the wild horsewomen of the air, coursing through storm clouds, whistling down the wind, lightning playing round their shields. It was marvellously effective. The role fitted von Richter's voice to perfection, her majestic physique appropriate to a daughter sprung from the Gods.

Siri shivered with excitement. A Wagnerian music drama demanded great voices, and the Baron-

61

ess had a great voice. There was no doubt about that. The powerful instrumentation, with its molten power and passion, was the work of genius.

The musicians in the pit were members of the Symphony Orchestra. She knew quite a few of them and they were all of them of the top rank. She divided her attention between Damian and the stage. It was a compelling performance, Wagner at his best.

After about ten minutes Damian broke off, bringing the cast to attention. 'Superb, Elisabeth. I think we'll go on to the Pleading. Other members of the cast may go. I will remind you that rehearsal begins this afternoon at two precisely. For now, Brunnhilde and Wotan on stage, please.'

The wild maidens of Valhalla took their departure with a great show of restraint, Siri thought. Damian gave them a few minutes, then brought down his hand on the orchestral passage introducing the great scene for soprano and bass. It had everything—beauty, nobility, tenderness, majesty and marvellous writing for the voice. Wotan was a magnificent hulk of a man with a voice to match and the range of a baritone.

Above the orchestra soared Brunnhilde, with some of the most brilliant and beautiful outpourings for dramatic soprano. Siri was thankful for the darkened stalls. The tears were damp on her cheeks. The scene rushed on to a glorious finale and the Baroness spoke over the footlights.

'It goes well, my dear?'

'Very much so, Lisa. I've never heard you in better voice.' St. Clair looked up at the smiling Wotan. 'You too, Hector. Your Wotan is extremely impressive.'

A sound came from the back of the theatre. St. Clair turned his dark head swiftly. 'Is that you, Miss Linton? Come down here, please.'

Siri got up at once, making her way towards the front of the stalls. She hoped the signs of recent tears were no longer apparent. They watched her approaching, her pallor pronounced against the midnight sheen of her hair, as it always was whenever she was aroused.

St. Clair turned to the diva, but she held up a shapely hand. 'But I know this young woman. Santuzza, is it not?'

'Serena Linton, Baroness.' Siri smiled into the tawny eyes. 'May I say I found the performance thrilling?'

The Baroness was disposed to be gracious. 'You may, my dear. May I present my colleague Hector Mainwaring?'

Siri smiled, 'How do you do, Mr. Mainwaring. Of course, I've heard you many times before.'

Hector bowed with dignity. 'Your protegée, St. Clair?' He looked full at the other man.

'Yes,' St. Clair answered unequivocally. 'I feel Miss Linton has operatic potential.'

The Baroness trilled into laughter. 'Come now, Damian my dear, with Miss Linton's voice and beauty, a great future, surely? I've never known you to waste your time. But for now you must excuse us. Hector insists on taking me to luncheon.' Her amber eyes lingered on the conductor.

'Santegelo this afternoon?'

'Yes, my dear. *Traviata*, the eternal crowd-pleaser.'

'Good, good, come along, my Wotan. I'm suddenly ravenous.' She swept off with a sweet condescending smile for Siri.

Hector Mainwaring picked up her gorgeous fur and spoke down to Siri. 'No doubt I'll be seeing more of you, Miss Linton?'

'Try and stop him,' Damian murmured *sotto voce.*

'I hope so.' Siri smiled up at the bass, then watched him make off after the Baroness. He drew the fur around her shoulders with lingering thoroughness.

St. Clair leaned back and looked at her. 'How goes it, child? And why the tears?'

I might have known he'd notice, Serena thought. 'Storm and stress,' she said aloud. 'Or the pitch of excitement. I'm very susceptible, you know.'

His eyes registered a black, sardonic amusement. 'Of course!'

'Thank you for letting me sit in on the rehearsal, Maestro. May I say I've never heard the orchestra sound richer or more sensuously beautiful?' She looked over at him with a sudden sense of affinity. His dark vitality with its imperious overtones flooded over her.

'You may, my child,' he answered lazily. 'But that's not all I wanted you here for. Our Sieglinde is pregnant, as an added touch of realism.'

Siri laughed at the very dry note of humour.

'It's no laughing matter, I assure you. I want you

64

to understand her as a precaution, but mainly Violetta. You know *Traviata*?'

She swallowed dryly. 'Yes, of course. But isn't that rather unusual? I mean. . . .' Her words died on her at the incredible hauteur of his face.

'I wasn't aware I had to fall in with the *usual*, Miss Linton. These are my productions. Just do as I say. Santegelo rehearses this afternoon, and just between the two of us and the rest of the world, she's a little past her prime.'

'How sad!' Siri said feelingly. 'So little time for us all.'

St. Clair drew a hand across his forehead, rather wearily. 'Don't remind me. Let's go somewhere quiet. A blessed interlude is what I need, with a beautiful, undemanding child.'

He flicked down his cuffs and refastened the gold links. Siri watched him adjust his tie with a feeling of fascination. He was immensely attractive. She picked up his jacket and held it for him, resisting the maddest inclination to rest her head against him, just lean against him for ever and ever and ever. She knew a moment of measureless hunger. But she was just like a silly schoolgirl with an outsize crush!

'I do believe you're learning,' he said cryptically. 'Those great eyes, they're positively unnerving. What are you thinking about, Siri?' His voice had an undercurrent of impatience.

'How right the performance was,' she lied easily. 'So outstandingly right and vital.' Her face gleamed in the half-light. 'So outstandingly right,' she repeated with unsmiling seriousness. The physical excitement of his presence was beginning to beset her.

'How much do you need taking in hand, I wonder?' His dark eyes held hers.

'How much?' she faltered.

'Yes, how much do you need me to guide you, Serena?'

'Are you sure you want to know?' She looked away.

'Of course. Don't dither.'

'Let me see.' Her expression suddenly changed from one of painful intensity to sheer impishness. 'I'm afraid you'll have to ask me again, Maestro. I'm not at all sure at the moment.'

'That's not the answer I required.' He made the slightest movement towards her and Siri flew away from him up the aisle with an unconscious look of challenge and defiance. He caught her up at the top.

'You of all people should be sure, Serena. You cannot, repeat, *cannot* succeed without me.' His voice was nicely calculated to topple all her self-confidence.

She smiled with some wisdom and a knowledge of pain. 'You frighten me, my dear Maestro. But even with your divine patronage my success is not a foregone conclusion.'

A lean, strong hand closed on the unprotected nape of her neck. 'I never undertake a venture I'm incapable of handling, my very dear Miss Linton. Lesson number one—in the theatre, self-confidence is more than half the battle.'

'Well, it's an interesting theory, Maestro, but only a theory,' she managed flippantly, then muffled a cry of pain. 'Oh, Damian, you hurt me.' There was an involuntary quality in her voice, a pleading with him. She was barely conscious of using his first name.

'I meant to, my lamb,' he said idly. 'You bring out the brute in me.' There was a faint smile in his eyes as though he was aware of her defencelessness. 'I suppose I must make allowances for your emotional fragility. Build yourself a protective shell if you must. Make it as high and as strong as you like, but it won't make the slightest difference. I have my own way in everything.'

Her face grew remote, enigmatic. 'Perhaps in five years when you've made me famous I won't mind so much.' She glanced at him from under her long lashes.

His brief laugh answered her and his look of unquestioned arrogance. So that was to be the way of it? Siri thought. But she had no intention of submitting so easily. Why should he be permitted this high-handed mastery? She had something of her own to contribute—her own precious talent. He wasn't the sum total of her existence. She walked with him into the bright sunshine, her head tilted imperiously.

The afternoon's session was as stormy as the morning's had been serene. Santegelo had great temperament, but her vocal strength fell short of making it bearable. She was also vain, capricious, illogical and, on her off-days, flatted in her top register.

Today was an off-day. Her usual soaring top notes lacked freedom and occasionally wavered, while her low register was consistently weak. Nothing and no one could please her. She disagreed violently with St. Clair on interpretation, tempi, scenic deployment and lighting, at the same time perversely recognising his superior dramatic conception and marvellously inventive lighting. Twenty years in the tense, provocative, fiercely competitive world of opera had taken toll of her nervous system.

The glittering 'Sempre Libera' just did not glitter, and now Alfredo was trying to upstage her. And being successful in the attempt, Siri observed with strict impartiality. She sat in the stalls and sweated it out for the diva. Admittedly Santegelo was being very awkward, but St. Clair was not helping at all.

Wickedly sarcastic and short-tempered, he was making no attempt to establish rapport with his soprano, and where were his fabled persuasive powers? The sympathetic, mutually responsive atmosphere of the morning had gone up in the smoke of fiery tempers. The duet was a disaster. Alfredo, the New Zealand tenor, Julian Graham, was young and in splendid vocal condition and his top notes were holding Santegelo's to the point of exhaustion.

She broke off in a fine rage, flinging vitriol all over the stage. The cast were fascinated, not understanding a word of it. Some English emerged.

'Non posso! I tell you. I am not pleased, not pleased at all.'

Damian too was not pleased and at pains to show

68

it. 'My productions are not calculated to please everyone, Signora. Perhaps if we went on to Act III, you could then lie down.'

'*Disgrazia*!' she hurled at him. 'You insult me, *me* —Santegelo! I am not well. Out of voice. I cannot continue.' She turned on her heel and flung through the chorus and out to her dressing room where she dissolved into helpless sobbing.

Damian did not seem to mind in the least. 'Keep your positions, ladies and gentlemen. I see no reason why we should disperse, however indisposed our prima donna. I will not have a wasted afternoon and neither will my musicians, all of whom are hoping to be paid.' There was some laughter from the pit. 'Would the Signora's substitute take the stage, please?'

Siri resisted the strong impulse to faint. The Signora's substitute! That was she since before lunch. It was no time to dither, fall into a panic or cry off with, 'I can't possibly do it!' He *expected* her to do it. Not only that, but to his own fastidious requirements. Well, she could match him!

Siri felt the eyes bore into her as she took the stage, though under St. Clair there was no ensuing babble of voices.

'Serena Linton, ladies and gentlemen,' he announced very coolly, off-handedly. 'The Signora's understudy. Now, shall we take it from Alfredo's "*liabiamo*". Julian, if you please.'

The chorus came to attention and Alfredo launched into his drinking song, to be taken up by Violetta with the chorus joining in. Siri made the transformation before their eyes, becoming Violetta Valéry, courtesan, gay and beautiful, but touched with sorrow.

Her voice rang out vividly, filling the theatre. St. Clair was already perfecting her performance. There were nuances, gestures and movements to be corrected. Her facial expressions couldn't be bettered. His own face was taut with concentration. Siri sank back upon the lounge to recover from the convincing coughing spell that racked her. The scene was unfolding. Young Graham was a polished Alfredo, his portrayal of passionate involvement nicely calculated. Tall and blond, he was the perfect counterfoil to the raven-haired Violetta.

St. Clair brought the orchestra to a halt before Violetta's solo. 'Very effective, Julian. One or two minor points we'll go over later. Miss Linton, I want more than the usual superficial glitter from your next solo, more an all-compassing characterization. I see Violetta as meltingly feminine, beautiful without question, but poignant and death-haunted even through the brilliance of the *Sempre Libera*'. His voice grew hypnotic. 'You are lost in contemplation, gazing unseeingly in your wall mirror turning slowly on *"Ah, fors e lui"*—for him perchance my longing soul!'

Her heart touched for the first time, Violetta began her aria with its passionate second section. Her sudden change into the dashing *Sempre Libera*' was well-judged; her voice and interpretive powers became fully apparent to the rest of the cast. All the time she was singing, St. Clair was working on her performance. In some places the voice was too strong. Her stage personality, even without the aid of proper make-up, was already effective. Her looks shone magnetically over the footlights; in the romantic costume of the period she would be ravishing. One performance before the public was all that she needed, and he would see that she got it. Violetta was the perfect vehicle at this stage of her career. She would learn and grow with every performance. As he had pointed out to her at their first meeting, her intensive pianistic training had ensured meticulous attention to the composer's wishes; her regard for the dynamic markings of the score, impeccable. All the elements of dramatic insight were there. He had only to channel her resources.

The cadenzas sparkled, each note sounding with clarity. He had Madame Castelli to thank for that. He would confine himself to the closest possible integration between singing and acting, to instilling the many fine nuances of stagecraft. She was only at the beginning.

At the end of the aria, the cast broke into spontaneous and emphatic applause, bringing the Italian diva out on to the stage with the speed of a gazelle. She had been watching from the wings.

'So, Miss Linton, is it?' Her voice was saccharine with restrained hostility. 'How kind of you to stand in for me, but now I am recovered and able to go on with the rehearsal. Maestro?' She directed a fiery glance at her one-time mentor.

St. Clair bowed with exaggerated courtesy. 'We are all of us glad to have you return, Signora. Whenever you're ready.' He dismissed Siri, his voice expressionless. 'Thank you, Miss Linton, you may go.'

'I have no living rival for my Violetta,' Santegelo was informing Alfredo, who was making no effort to hide his resentment over what he plainly considered an outrageous lie, especially in the face of the last performance. The lovely Miss Linton had lifted his performance to the air. Santegelo merely depressed him.

The rehearsal continued, but without Siri. The bitter exchanges were for later.

CHAPTER SIX

THE week of rehearsal preceding the season was hectic. Siri had perfected her Sieglinde but had no occasion to try it out on stage. Rosalind Vaughan, the soprano who had been assigned the role, might have been pregnant, but she was keeping amazingly well, especially for the early stages, and was in fact the only one of the two to have any sense of anticipation at all. Siri felt reasonably sure she would never be called on as the emergency substitute.

She and Clive did find a considerable amount of work from among the cast as vocal coaches and accompanists. Hector Mainwaring had even approached her to run through some of his arias, or so he said. He was to play Germont, Alfredo's father, in the *Traviata* production. Siri was glad of a legitimate excuse. She was far too busy, but referred him to Clive, who not having the necessary flawless ivory complexion, heard no more of it. Charlotte had enjoyed Siri's telling of the encounter. The amorous bass had been delighted with himself, and because of it utterly charming, patting Siri's face as he put his question. Siri's decline had brought him up short, but not for long. He had stormed unassailable citadels before this.

Of Damian she saw surprisingly little outside of rehearsals. There he was a human dynamo, radiating energy and excitement. Forceful and original, he kept the whole cast at the peak of their powers, whipped into shape by his theatrical flair and his all-powerful baton.

The productions were crystallising well. The Baroness was a tireless Brunnhilde, always in splendid voice and seemingly without temperament, while even the tempestuous Santegelo had painstakingly perfected her roles of Violetta, Amina, and Mimi.

It was towards the end of the Wednesday evening rehearsal that Clive came into the theatre to collect Siri. She had been covertly watching Damian, who was in intense conversation with his two Wagnerian leads. His face was vivid, almost elated, lit up with ideas from an inexhaustible reservoir. The Baroness was leaning towards him, one shapely hand on his shoulder, her handsome face alight with more than artistic response. Theirs had been a splendid collaboration, as the public would be witness to.

Siri felt an upsurge of unfamiliar jealousy. As though he were conscious of her regard Damian turned abruptly, his brilliant gaze flashing some sort of message to her. Siri chose to ignore it.

Clive threaded his way through the little groups of singers who were holding post-mortems, the musicians propped up smoking the cigarettes forbidden to the singers, and on to Siri, his sensitive face lighting up as he caught sight of her. Siri regarded him with affection. She was very fond of him. His nature was as deep and as loving as his music.

'Siri beloved, I am here, late but not lost. Are you ready?' He looked round for her music-case.

'I hope you're not leaving, Serena. There are several things I want to discuss with you.'

Damian nodded pleasantly to Clive. 'Good evening, Martyn. The Baroness has just been echoing your praises. She found your accompanying most sympathetic.'

Clive blushed with pleasure. 'It was a great honour for me.'

Siri felt vaguely resentful, and woman-like didn't know the exact cause for it.

Clive looked hesitatingly from one to the other. 'Shall I wait, Siri?'

'Of course not.' Damian cut across her. 'Go along, get your rest. I'll see to Siri.'

'Well, then——' Clive looked a little doubtful. 'I'll see you tomorrow, Siri. Good night, sir.'

Siri waited a moment, then left Damian standing. Her music case was out in the hall somewhere. She found it easily.

'Really, Siri, do I detect something new in your attitude? A certain veiled hostility?' He moved with the grace of a panther and as much menace, effectively blocking her way.

'Do we have your discussion here?' Siri looked up at him with cool hauteur.

He said nothing but took her face between his hands, tipping her head back. Her eyes were great shadowy pools, giving little hint of her inner turmoil.

'Not unless you want to, Siri,' he said dangerously. She drew a sharp breath, her body knowing a reflex action of escape. It communicated itself to him through his nerve centres. 'Keep still, girl. What are you afraid of? That I'll make love to you?'

'Perhaps.' She was breathless.

'Then you're doomed to disappointment. You'll have to go down on your knees and beg for it.' Some emotion was smouldering in his eyes, ready to fan into flame. A nerve beat in the smooth bronze temple.

'My first lesson was quite enough, thank you, Maestro,' Siri murmured unsteadily. 'May I be permitted to pass?'

His arms fell away. 'Why, certainly, you ungrateful little wretch!' His smile was rather condescending for St. Clair. 'I'll be finished here in about ten minutes. Then perhaps we can go somewhere. . . . oh, anywhere you like. I don't care to eat alone.'

Siri stood, the picture of uncertainty. What was it he wanted of her? This eternal cat and mouse game! In the end, of course, he decided where they would go—late supper at Corelli's. Siri was a little unhappy. Her topcoat was very chic, but even so she wasn't dressed for such an exclusive restaurant. She said so.

He ran the hard eye of the expert over her. 'You're joking, darling,' he drawled sarcastically. 'Black is your colour—or rather, lack of colour. The stark setting is quite shattering, believe me.'

Siri looked up and found the sensual mouth mocking. He was no more amusing himself with a helpless unknown. A young singer of no consequence. . . .

Corelli's was luminous with lights, the atmosphere intimate and romantic. Heads turned recognising him, and Siri determined to throw off her mounting tension. She was really very tired, and Damian excited and baffled her. He seemed to sense her mood, for he set out to put her at ease. His manner grew nicely impersonal with just the faintest hint of awareness. He watched her relax with something like amusement. She was very susceptible, for all her guarded heart.

Siri, hypersensitive to mood, felt somehow stranded. There was an undercurrent of tension beneath the lazy banter, the charm that she could not withstand. Tonight, at least, she was determined not to be ensnared by him. But she enjoyed herself very much, after she gave up trying to resist his flagrant charm.

Damian St. Clair was a creature of the night, as she was, at home and thriving in the lush urban world of neon lights. He was witty and charming, slightly aloof yet tantalising, vaguely patronising as befitting a man in his position. When they left the restaurant the stars were shimmering above the brilliantly lit street. It was cold and she shivered. He took her arm and walked her to where the Mercedes was parked.

The bright conversation of supper had given way to a vivid silence. He drove fast and expertly out of the city. When he finally pulled up on a headland overlooking the harbour, Siri felt the tears prick under her eyelids.

His voice turned her heart over. 'Come here, *cara*

mia!' She couldn't move and he turned her towards him, his beautiful hands sure and steady.

It was like going over the rapids, this turmoil in the blood; this violent assault on the sense. A great wind rushed through her head and he began kissing her, round her mouth, her eyes, her ears and the delicate hollow at the base of her throat, until Siri, half delirious with yearning, caught his mouth with her own.

Every bone in her body had melted. It was unlike any lovemaking she had ever imagined, even thought possible! Her blood was on fire and she longed only for the moments to extend, endlessly, endlessly, enveloped by the night. She spoke against his lean cheekbone, her breath coming unevenly. 'Why do you do it? You told me I would have to beg for it.' There was a long silence. 'Please,' she said breathlessly, 'you promised.'

His laugh was soft, self-mocking. 'Which just goes to show you can't trust me. I'm only a man, and you're a rather beautiful child. I'd be a fool to resist such a heaven-sent opportunity.'

A hurt cry escaped her. 'And that's all it is to you? A chance opportunity?'

His eyes narrowed at her look of desperate uncertainty. 'And what more should it be?' he drawled, watching her closely. 'Tell me, Siri.'

She was silent, waiting for the pressures inside her to lessen.

He gave a brief laugh. 'You take life too seriously, my babe. Hasn't your Clive kissed you? He seems so very loving.'

'He hasn't as yet,' she replied jerkily, not knowing how best to answer him.

'And will he?'

She caught his expression and thought it ruthless and mocking. 'Perhaps,' she managed airily. 'Who can say? You yourself are the arch-advocate for experience.'

He caught her face, twisting it up to him. 'Perhaps I may want your exclusive favours.'

'For the run of the performance,' she flung at him scathingly. 'Really, for all your suave façade you're the Neanderthal type, aren't you?'

His eyes glittered with malice. 'The answer to that is simple. I'm not quite so primitive, my child. And aren't *you* lucky? You respond a little too well for your own safety.'

She smoothed her ruffled hair and she thought helplessly: I'm completely and utterly and hopelessly lost to him. I must do something about it, for my own self-respect.

'I'd like to go home now,' she said tautly. 'I'm well aware I'm out of my league.'

He sighed in the darkness. 'Yes, you are, dear, aren't you! Ah well, I suppose I'd better oblige, seeing your frightened young heart is making difficulties.' He leaned forward and switched on the ignition, his dark eyes glittering in the light from the dash. 'You only *think* you know what I am and what I want from you. You have a long way to go before you can play the game.'

Tears sparkled diamond-bright on her long eyelashes. He caught the sheen of them. 'Don't try a

79

little emotional blackmail. It won't work at all. You're a big enough headache as it is. Now come along, dry your eyes and I'll take you home, little girl.' His voice, light and sarcastic, was still touched with a fleeting tenderness.

CHAPTER SEVEN

SIRI opened out the shutters on the soft, bright morning. The light struck at her bedazzled eyes, banishing the last trace of sleep. She shook back the heavy plait from her face and gazed over the sill. An industrious spider was busy weaving a pattern from the sill to the low-flowering crimson azaleas. The cobweb, catching the reflection of the late winter sunlight, looked to be made of gold.

What a heavenly morning! The shafted sun lay in a lengthening arch across the wet garden, multiplying to eternity the shimmering, shivering dewdrops. The birds had been up for hours, chirruping in the dappled-leaf sunshine. It was on mornings like these when one felt one could do almost anything!

Siri turned away and dashed into her usual routine; ten minutes' deep breathing and exercise, followed by a shower. St. Clair would be here before lunch to run through *Traviata*, though why he should choose to spend a weekend rehearsing a part she would be unlikely to play for years yet was more than she could fathom. The last two days of rehearsal had been non-stop for all the cast. The Wagnerian Ring Cycle was to open on the following Wednesday and run through the three successive nights until Saturday.

One would have thought that even the great St.

Clair deserved some rest and relaxation, but apparently he had no such thoughts! He arrived about ten, stopping to talk to Charlotte who was already busy with her precious plants. The two of them bent their heads to a minute inspection.

He continued up the path and Siri went out to meet him, her heart leaping wildly. 'Good morning, Maestro. I didn't know you were an authority on spring bulbs.'

He looked at her with relaxed insolence. 'You obviously can't be expected to know everything about me, can you?' His eyes suddenly flickered. 'Damn! I've forgotten the parcel. I'll have to go back to the car.' He swerved away from her and out to the car, pausing to say something to Charlotte. Her peal of laughter carried on the breeze.

The parcel turned out to be a crinoline gown borrowed from Wardrobe. If Siri was to rehearse her role, she must do it in costume, not only to feel herself into the role, but to become accustomed to wearing the hooped skirt of the period. Damian walked back into the house and threw the box down on the lounge chair.

'Five minutes,' he said, characteristically terse, and walked to the music-room.

Siri shut the door on her bedroom and opened the box with a mixture of curiosity and eagerness. An incredibly frothy confection of white tulle, taffeta and lace foamed out at her. She held it up and out. The tiny off-the-shoulder bodice had flounces falling to the elbow, heavily embroidered with silver, while the skirt was enormous, embroidered with silver scrolls and the floral motif of the encrusted sleeves. Wonder of wonders, it fitted!

Somewhere she had read that one should walk pigeon-toed to obtain the correct sway of the hoops. She immediately turned her toes in and tried it. The skirt certainly swayed, but was it alluring? She felt slightly ridiculous, but no one would see her feet. Damian would know. She went out to him with her new walk.

'Well, I'd die waiting for a reaction from you,' Siri said, her head on one side looking at him quizzically.

'You surprise me, child. I rather had the impression you'd die if you *did* get a reaction from me. However, your Violetta has the necessary fragility. You look very well, Miss Linton, as if there was an instant's doubt you had about it.'

'Oh, God, you're a sarcastic beast,' she said jerkily, her stormy face at odds with her gown.

'Now, now, no tantrums.' He held up a hand. 'From the beginning, Violetta ...'

For once they were in rapport, rehearsing endlessly, equally fastidious with painstaking attention to minutiae. Siri's voice fully met the technical demands of the role, but it was the interpretation St. Clair was so interested in. Violetta was such a damned elusive role! He made a few significant changes, then set about refining gestures and movements. Siri followed his direction easily, deferring to his vastly superior judgment.

They both started when Charlotte knocked at the door. 'Do you two propose stopping for lunch, or are you going to make a welter of it?'

'A welter of it, Charlotte? What could you mean?' Damian got to his feet and stretched his long arms to the ceiling. He smiled rather sardonically at the girl leaning against the piano. 'I think we're meant to have lunch, if such an ethereal creature eats lunch.'

'She certainly does,' Charlotte answered for her. 'Come along, you two. I want some company too, you know.' She circled Siri, admiring the white gown. 'You look gorgeous, love. Ghastly days for women, of course. But the costume! You look quite fictitious.'

Siri smiled. 'What have you prepared for us? I don't *feel* fictitious!'

'It's nothing elaborate,' Charlotte laughed, 'but I think you'll like it. Come along and see.'

She led them through to the sun-porch where she had set up the table. Through the huge bay window one could see all over the terraced garden and the rockery which Charlotte had worked so hard to create. In spring it was covered with an astonishing range of colour and even now trails of ivy covered the rough stone with a background of camellias and low-growing azaleas. Further down the hillside a magnificent wattle was in full, beautiful bloom.

Siri listened to her aunt, who was discussing soil types and suitable plants with her distinguished visitor, as though it was in no way unusual, and she smiled to herself and walked off to change the gown. Now that they had finished working she was cold around the arms and shoulders.

Lunch was an entertaining affair with no shop talk whatever, if you discounted how to drain a difficult site. With the encouragement and inspiration of the morning, Siri threw herself into being amusing. Charlotte observed Damian from the corner of her eye. No one so brilliant and exciting had ever swum into their ken. But he was incalculable. A woman would do well to beware of him. She saw his brilliant gaze dwell briefly on Siri and she knew a moment's fear for her new-born lamb.

After lunch, they returned to rehearsing. There was the vital third act to be gone through. The final aria was not to his wishes. He took pains to correct it.

'Too strong, Siri. Remember, Violetta has sensed the near approach of death.'

She tried again and he held up an impatient hand.

'I know you're singing *piano*, but I want it even softer, a floating quality. You can do it. I've heard you. The correct interpretive spirit could be likened to a sigh from the depths of a soul purified by a great and ennobling love. Try it once more.'

The voice started again but this time *pianissimo*, but carrying beautifully, palpitating with sorrow. They went through it again and again until it was second nature. And so it went on until late afternoon. Charlotte had come in to light the fire and walked out without so much as interrupting the flow of the duet. She smiled to herself, richly amused. Had he been a singer, Damian would undoubtedly have been a baritone. Those top notes were left to a sweeping lift of the hand. They would have to stop soon. He was giving an orchestral concert at the City Hall that evening. How did he do it? she asked herself. He appeared to be inexhaustible, making no differentiation between work and pleasure.

The birds of the air were making their last turn round in the declining light before he called it a day. Damian looked up at Siri. She had her back to the light, her head framed in dark tresses, her eyes resting on him. Her skin had become invested with rosy incandescence from the fire behind her. It found a bright reflection in the depths of his eyes. For a moment she was afraid to move or to speak, do anything to disturb her feeling of other-worldliness. A log spluttered and fell into the grate.

Siri stirred and laughed. 'For a moment there, I'd gone off to an indescribably beautiful planet inhabited by just the two of us, and now I'm back again.'

He stood up with abrupt grace. 'Sometimes you say the damnedest things. I don't even think you give a thought to their consequences.'

She blinked her eyelashes, disturbed by his tone. When would she ever learn not to go around speaking her thoughts aloud?

'I don't understand you,' she said defensively.

He glanced at her briefly. 'And why should you? Your experience of the jungle is minimal, as I've told you before.' He shot back his cuff. 'Good grief, is that the time? I'm cutting it very fine. Where's

Charlotte?'

'Waiting outside, I expect.'

'You're coming tonight?' He shot the question at her from under frowning brows.

'I thought that was understood, Maestro.'

'Nothing's understood with you, Miss Linton. Now, I really must go.'

Charlotte was in the hallway, holding his coat for him. 'All ready? What a beautiful coat, Damian. Superb tailoring.'

He shrugged into it. 'As only the English can do it. Australian wool, if we're going to give the home country a boost.'

'Ah well, we're all much of a muchness!' Charlotte said comfortably. She turned to her niece. 'Does the gown stay?'

'Only until Monday. Isn't that right, Maestro?' Siri tilted her head to him.

He nodded absently, seemingly preoccupied. 'Yes, bring it in with you, but walk around in it first. Get the feel of it, though you have the feel already, if the truth be known.' He turned to Charlotte with a smile. 'Walk out to the car with me. Stay here, Siri. The gown might get marked.'

'I had no intention of intruding,' Siri said pertly, and earned herself a glance of reprisal. She watched after them until the car pulled away. Charlotte lingered for a last look at her bulbs, so Siri went straight through to her room to change.

CHAPTER EIGHT

ANYBODY who was anybody attended the first night, including a whole lot of nobodies who somehow managed to exhibit better manners. Azure mink jostled with go-anywhere tweed, while ladies in meltaway chiffons swished beside the sumptuous splendour of satin and brocade. All of them in turn ogling the thinking, doing, going, hip crowd in an extravaganza of gear to satisfy the most blatant yen for originality. Those who had diamonds wore them. Those who didn't, rhinestones and lashings of beads.

With the prospect of a brilliant evening, ripples of laughter, born of bubbling spirits, circled the theatre and faces suffused with delight and surprise and cries of: 'Fancy seeing *you* here!' The whole atmosphere was redolent of perfume, anticipatory excitement and brisk flirtations before the curtain rose.

In the foyer the flash bulbs were blinding with society smiles just as easily switched on. It was a flying, gliding cartwheel of colour. Those that were in town and weren't musically minded turned out in front of the theatre to clap and have a look at the gala dressing. It was more than a typical first night crowd. It was a great occasion!

Siri settled for the patrician look; an asymmetrical toga of black velvet over a column of white silk crêpe. It was very soft, very sleek and completely alluring. Enormous triangular earrings in jet and silver swung from her ears and her hair was arranged in great shining coils. Heads swung in her direction.

Charlotte wore her onyx green brocade with its beautiful matching evening coat and Madame Castelli was swathed in a lamé creation, so old-fashioned it was the last gasp! She stood just inside the main doors, volubly holding court. Her face was vivid with overtones of her glittering youth and if her accent sometimes made her conversation unintelligible, her charm bridged all barriers.

An ancient, withered lady in green satin with black velvet tied around her neck wandered through the foyer, going from group to group without actually settling on anybody. She was causing considerable interest and some sniggers. The warning bell called them all to their seats. Inside the theatre, the elegant, the intelligentsia, the students, the tourists, all settled back in their expensive seats, sharing the wonderful feeling of being able to afford the most brilliant and highest-priced entertainment of the season. They also shared a blissful ignorance of the furore backstage.

Dressers hurried hither and thither with costumes in their arms. Men shifted flats with singers still leaning against them, silently vocalising. The theatre was filled to capacity. In the proscenium box sat the Governor and his lady, who was in ermine. It was extraordinarily exciting. And what of the city's own Damian St. Clair? How would they greet him?

The answer came as he entered the orchestra pit. The audience came to their feet for a two-minute standing ovation, a massive display of their pride and affection. He bowed to their prolonged applause.

Das Rheingold opened with its wonderfully evocative prelude, all the quietude of the water depths, the home of the Rhine-maidens. The horn intoned the Rhine Motif, one horn after another taking it up in its wave-like motion, rising higher and higher with the strings joining in, until the theme stirred the waters to the depths and the curtain rose.

A sound made up of dozens of oohs! and aahs! greeted the staging; the new settings were superb. Siri swallowed hard. She was becoming over-stimulated. The ovation for St. Clair had moved her to tears. Through the four scenes the audience became totally involved with the supernatural beings of German mythology. The Baroness, as Brunnhilde, would not appear until the following night in *Die Walküre*, but the resident Australian sopranos who sang the roles of the goddesses were complete artists. Hector Mainwaring as Wotan appeared in all four dramas. He was giving a splendid performance.

A bright golden light bathed the stage to the shimmering accompaniment of the violins and the Rhinegold motif rang out brilliantly on the trumpet. The Rhine daughters' shout of triumph was invested with great power, echoing through the theatre. The orchestration was tremendous, and the musicians in the pit rose to it under such authoritative baton.

As the drama was brought to a close, the applause crashed down on the artists. They had had their money's worth and so, extraordinarily enough, had the critics. There was an ensemble curtain call, then one for Wotan and his goddesses, and another for Wotan. Then there were clamorous calls for the conductor, and Damian took the stage, his sardonic good looks, Siri considered, as inscrutable as ever.

Afterwards there was the usual stampede for the late night suppers arranged here, there and everywhere. In the foyer there were cascades of highly appreciative comment. The old lady who had caused so much comment earlier in the evening stood with a tall, very stern old gentleman, weighed down with medals and various decorations. As Charlotte and Siri passed, they heard her speaking. Her voice was thin, but cultured and sane, engaged in an erudite discussion on the *Gotterdammerung*. As she lifted her hand, an enormous, square-cut emerald flashed green fire at them.

'Well, well!' said Charlotte. 'Still waters run deep. Our mystery lady is very much a lady, despite the quaint costume.'

Siri looked genuinely startled. 'Whoever supposed she was not?' She had thought nothing amiss. Old ladies were characters and she liked them, allowed them their eccentricities.

Charlotte looked at her eagerly. 'Shall we go backstage and congratulate Damian? I'm sure he expects us.'

Siri put a detaining hand on her arm. 'Let's leave him, Lottie. He'll be surrounded by socialites, snobs and sycophants.'

'Even so, dear!' Charlotte remonstrated, but Siri was not to be moved. She felt, among other things, unduly sensitive about intruding on his moment of glory and for that she brought down wrath on their heads. The telephone was ringing urgently as they let themselves into the house. Siri walked to it with a presentiment of anger.

'Siri, you graceless little wretch! You'd better have a good explanation!'

'Explanation?' she protested, watching Charlotte shake her head in instant comprehension.

'Yes, explanation ... *excuse*, damn you. Don't act so stupidly, for God's sake. Oh, to hell with it!' he broke off wrathfully. 'I'm coming out! I should have thought Charlotte would have enough social sense for the two of you.' He hung up furiously in her ear.

'He's coming out,' Siri said, appalled.

'We're in for it, aren't we?' Charlotte didn't look in the least perturbed. She had had years of this kind of temperament. 'Don't worry, he'll have cooled off by the time he arrives.' She looked over at Siri, who was standing stock still in the best tragedy queen tradition. 'You did the wrong thing, child. I knew it. You knew it. But why? Oh, never mind, I don't suppose you know yourself.'

She hurried away to prepare a supper. *Head them off with something appetising!* That was her motto. By training and temperament, Charlotte concealed a lot of her thoughts and feelings, but she just might have a word with Damian. Siri was building herself some sort of a shelter. It was understandable. His was such a dominant personality and Siri's had not fully emerged. It was a form of protection, a need to assert the inviolable self. Charlotte busied herself in the kitchen, humming snatches of the evening's programme.

Siri heard the car pull up at the front of the house and went out to meet him, more to bear the brunt of his displeasure than anything else, she told herself.

He was cool and suave with a note of formality. 'Ah, Serena, my dear child! How charming of you to come out to meet me.'

Her eyes widened. This she had not expected!

'You white witch!' He reached for her suddenly, spinning her off balance. Her earrings swung wildly against her cheekbones. In the faint light from the garden lamp he had a hard, glittering look that further unnerved her.

'Come now, Siri, I'm waiting. Why the calculated rebuff? Even from you I didn't expect it.' The coolness had given way to subdued violence.

'But I thought you were wonderful, too wonderful,' she whispered, distraught. 'I wanted to get away from you. You're overwhelming. You obsess me. I don't know what to do about it!'

'You obsess me too, you little fool, and I don't like it either. Not one little bit!' His mouth came down on hers, forcing it open with wilful, uncontrollable passion and fury. Strong, lean hands encircled her throat, forcing her to accept his demands, until, too shattered for further resistance, Siri flowed into him, young and desirable.

He moved her back into the scented shadows, with the night blooming around them. His mouth moved down the ivory column of her neck and rested in the silken hollow at his base. 'Such mysterious powers a witch has,' he muttered with barely concealed male resentment.

Her voice stayed him. 'Please, Damian. Charlotte will have heard the car. We must go up to the house. Will all our discussions end like this?' she asked almost plaintively.

He lifted his head, shaking it slightly. 'Centuries ago, my dear, they would undoubtedly have burnt you. And probably a good thing.'

She looked up at him helplessly, trying to fathom his baffling, tormenting expression. 'You're crazy!' she said inadequately.

'Could I be mistaken and you really are stupid under that beautiful exterior?' His hands tightened 'I'm far from crazy, yet you have a certain fascination for me. Make what you like of it.'

'You surely couldn't mean *marriage*.' She stumbled over the enormity of the word. As usual, it had presented itself unbidden.

'My God!' He hit a hand to his forehead. 'Did I say anything about marriage? The very sound of the word depresses me to the point of tears. A man barely has time to count to three before one of you Aphrodites whips him to the altar, trapped for life. I've had far too many narrow escapes already.'

Siri seemed to find this terribly funny. 'Good grief!' she burst out, 'surely you didn't think I was serious? Why, I'd be the last woman in the world to deprive you of your love-starred—*starred*, I said, not *starved*—freedom.'

'Love-*starred*,' he repeated mercilessly. 'Are you seriously referring to me? I've never ever said I've been in love, you idiot girl. Do try to speak to me with the voice of intelligence.'

She pulled away from him in a passion. 'Next you'll be telling me I'm the first girl you've kissed!'

His hands caught her fast. 'If you don't stop this lunacy, you'll be the first girl I've choked,' he murmured with imminent violence.

'Damian, Siri! Do you ever intend to come up?' Charlotte called to them, an unmistakable thread of anxiety in her voice.

'Coming, Lottie,' Siri answered, and fled on ahead. Charlotte stood back for them, shutting the door quietly. She reached up and kissed Damian's cheek. 'You were marvellous, my dear. I was so proud of you. Like an eagle soaring above the rest of us.' She looked from one to the other. 'And been acting like one too, I gather.'

Damian put an arm around her shoulder. 'Soothe me, Charlotte. Soothe me, for God's sake. Siri drives me to distraction with her moods and caprices. I've never encountered such a perverse, illogical and archaically-minded young woman.'

Charlotte laughed, only half understanding, and led them through to the dining room while Siri took the opportunity to freshen her lipstick. Her

eyes were enormous and quite brilliant, hectic unaccustomed colour shading her cheekbones. In her
classical gown she looked more than ever an en-
chantress, but a deeply bewildered one. How could
she have mentioned marriage? What a fool she
was! It was the furthest thing from her mind. Yet
he provoked these answers. She had never so much
as given him an instant's encouragement. He had
made all the advances—and such advances! Her
cheeks flamed. And then he had denied his love life
when the glossy magazines and the musical periodi-
cals splashed his handsome face throughout their
pages, always accompanied by some sparkling companion from the world of the theatre of society. At
best they were drawn by a blind chemistry. At
worst, a mutual antagonism that could not be denied. Oh, damn! Siri threw a tissue at her own
reflection. Why bother to hide it? She had loved
him when she had first seen him, she loved him
now, and even being what he was, she would undoubtedly always love him.

There was a tap at the door, bringing her out of
her trancelike reflections. She moved swiftly over
the dull gold carpet and threw open the door.
Damian stood there, looking down at her, his dark
eyes glimmering with mockery.

'Had you intended to lock your door against me?'

'Why would I bother? I'm quite sure you would
only knock it down.'

He studied her for a moment. 'If it were only
that simple, Serena. Come along, you tiresome
child. Charlotte has made the supper, seeing you

96

are in no way domesticated, and I have brought the champagne.' He caught her arm. 'Don't stalk past me like a panther, if you don't mind.'

'A panther?' She stopped in her tracks, looking at him in astonishment.

'Well, a cat lady at least.' His lean arrogant face was full of sardonic amusement.

She made a tremendous effort to combat his magnetic attraction for her. What was so maddening was that he seemed to be aware of it.

'Damian—' Charlotte's voice reached them easily, 'do come and open the champagne for me.'

Damian laughed. 'You heard, Siri. Come drink to the success of the performance, if nothing else. Out of the scores of people who congratulated me you seem to be the one who sticks in my mind.'

All at once, she was conscience-stricken. She was detracting from the pleasure of his own personal triumph. Her aloof air vanished, leaving her beautiful eyes wonderfully soft and expressive.

'I'm sorry,' she said simply. 'I'm really in great awe of you. I didn't mean to slight you in any way, especially tonight. Your brilliance is quite intimidating.'

He smiled slightly. 'Never to you, Siri. You're only waiting to get into your stride. Then there'll be no holding you. Still, I wouldn't have you any other way.' Devilment lurked in his eyes. 'A curtain between my past and my present.'

What struck her most was the brilliance of his eyes, at once sardonic and brimming with laughter.

97

'Come now, child, working among temperamental divas all day I detest scenes and theatricalities. I deeply regret my past follies and wickednesses, whatever they may be. I want only to shield you from them, my hopeless innocent.'

The beautiful wild rose colour sprang to her face. 'It's a mistake to pander to you, isn't it?' She swept past him with a wonderfully scornful air, but he was quicker.

He barred her way very effectively. 'I'm going to bring you to heel, or die in the attempt.'

The soft concealed lighting lent the even, ivory pallor of her smooth skin a deceptive tranquillity. Silent tears of frustration filled her eyes. 'I'll never, never, never give in!' she whispered quite vehemently.

'Oh yes, you will, you self-willed, self-opinionated, romantically inclined little cat.' His voice was filled with amiable malice.

Charlotte appeared at the end of the hallway. Damian withdrew his hand from the wall, coming to attention. 'Divine intervention! Siri had me trapped here in an extremely invidious position.'

'Stop teasing now, Damian,' Charlotte said soothingly. 'Siri darling, come along and take your place. You've had nothing all day, to the best of my knowledge.'

Damian followed in Charlotte's wake, mildly malicious once more. 'Now that *is* a pathetic situation!'

Siri ignored him, but every fibre in her body was

tingling. She would teach him a lesson, she vowed to herself. Not every woman was fair game for the great Damian St. Clair. She had it in her to be very clever!

CHAPTER NINE

SIRI, as Sieglinde's emergency substitute, was required backstage for the performance of *Die Walküre*, bringing her to Hector Mainwaring's immediate attention. She was standing amid the props, reading through the numerous glowing accounts of the first night which Rosalind Vaughan had added to her scrapbook, when she felt someone start breathing down her neck with bloodcurdling effect. Siri swung round, only to bring herself up against the massive chest of Hector in his guise of the highly amatory god.

'Well met, Miss Linton.'

Siri tried to smile and stepped back precipitately, catching her foot in some stage equipment. Hector moved with commendable agility and caught her back up against him, smiling with an effect which could only be described as rich masculinity. Siri tried demurely to work herself loose, but to no effect. He seemed to be reading something into her playful struggles which was not at all intended. She threw back her head, her eyes glinting at him.

'I have a feeling you're taking advantage of me, sire. It's rather ungenerous.'

His smile deepened, more flattered than not. 'Beneath the rose lurks a thorn,' he murmured silkily, and loosened his hold, but not entirely.

'I don't quite accept that. But since you've mentioned it, are you going to unhand me?'

The thick reddish brown eyebrows came together in reproof. 'But you are so unkind, Miss Linton. Why, you silly child,. you and I could share a very tender friendship.'

His lips began to pucker and Siri felt irritation beginning to get the better of her. She had a decided ache in the small of her back.

'I don't think Miss Linton is sharing your affection, Hector. But then you can't win 'em all!' St. Clair was casually observing them. The bass let Siri go and turned around, completely at ease and good-tempered.

'You can hardly blame me for trying. I mean, damn it, Damian, you've got quite a reputation yourself. Miss Linton is exquisite, but so prim, so proper. Such a clear head too for inciting men to madness.'

Siri laughed and arched her delicate black brows. 'You make too much of a charming piece of nonsense, sire!'

Hector's eyes brightened. There was a fine nuance in her voice that seemed to be egging him on. He was alive to such things. He felt his heart begin to beat violently, but he carefully avoided touching the lovely young thing. St. Clair had a look of sardonic appreciation, but a certain hard watchfulness. 'How could you interrupt us, Damian, and we were doing so terribly well.' He made a droll face at St. Clair. 'But never mind, it's only the start of the season, eh, Miss Linton, or I will say—Serena.'

Her eyes were downcast, but she was smiling. Hector bowed with some majesty and took himself back to his dressing room, not a little pleased with the encounter.

'And now you've been made love to by Wotan—' The dark eyes were provoking.

'By an orang-outan, more like it,' Siri said feelingly. 'He's terribly strong. Are all men so appallingly conceited? I really believe he thought I might enjoy a moment's dalliance among the backdrops.'

'And wouldn't you? It's not unheard of.'

Siri flushed. 'Apparently not. I heard what he said to *you*.'

'Never among the backdrops,' Damian drawled lazily, his black eyes flicking over her.

Her lashes made black fans on her cheeks. 'Such delicacy!' she said lightly. 'Wine, woman and song and perish the thought of tomorrow.'

He laughed, a great deal amused. The Baroness followed the direction of that laugh. She swept up to them in the magnificent garb of the Valkyrie. Siri moved back for her. 'You look splendid, Baroness. I'm sure your performance will match it.'

'Why, thank you, child.' The Baroness was pleased by the girl's obvious sincerity. 'Your moment will come,' she promised benignly. 'Damian, my dear—' She rested a hand on his shoulder. They were of a height with her helmet on, and he topped six feet. 'There is a small irritation only you can correct.' She hesitated for a moment and Siri tactfully excused herself. Now what could it be? She had never seen anyone quite like the Baroness before. She stood perfectly calm, tall, grave and handsome, completely occupied in telling Damian the small irritation. No trace of pre-performance nerves was apparent, if indeed she suffered from them. Siri smiled to herself. There would be no discrepancy between the conception and the reality of tonight's Brunnhilde.

'And what do you imagine you are doing *camping* here?' a voice said caustically. The Signora Santegelo had come backstage to wish her colleague well. The sight of the pretentious Miss Linton was enough to invoke a cold fury, especially as she had nearly cannoned into her, being so confoundedly shortsighted.

'Why, yes, Signora, and I've only just begun.' Siri gave her back look for look, noting the uncontrollable antagonism.

'You are very rude indeed, Signorina.' The Italian diva swept past with a look of fiery insolence. She was dead white and the hand holding her beautiful fur was shaking. Siri looked after her with an expression of dismay. Santegelo looked as if she was on the verge of a breakdown, or she had worked up a considerable hate for one who was really at this stage quite beneath her notice. Siri for all her great talent had little vanity and failed to grasp how quick the diva had been to scent a strong rival.

When the curtain rose on the evening's performance, Siri felt as though a great weight had fallen from her shoulders. It was quite nerve-racking backstage, especially when you had nothing of value to contribute. But from then on she was fascinated and couldn't tear herself away from the wings. Through Act I she sang silently with Sieglinde. She wasn't altogether happy with Rosalind's performance. It was too stately, too measured for white-hot burning passion. Spontaneity and abandon were lacking. Perhaps it was her condition— they did say pregnancy had a settling effect.

The orchestration was marvellous. Siri's palms pressed tightly together. The strings throbbed in unison with the hearts of the lovers.

'Oh, wondrous vision!

Rapturous woman!'

The action fairly seethed with excitement, brilliant like the glitter off Siegmund's sword.

The Love Motif rushed onwards to the height of passion as the curtain came down on Act I, with Siegmund holding the doomed Sieglinde in his embrace. The applause was warm with a quality of anticipation. Everyone was awaiting the German diva.... Act II and she was away, hurtling her battle cry to the gods. Siri thought that she looked magnificent under the lights. The costume was superb.

The Baroness was a superb dramatic soprano. There was no one to touch her for sheer volume and power, and the part of the youthful, vigorous Brunnhilde suited her personality to a T. But for Siri there was nothing to compare with the wild and lofty beauty of the last act, the great scene between Brunnhilde and Wotan.

Brunnhilde lay upon her rock, her helmet down, covered by her shield, surrounded by the magic flames which only the heroic Siegfried would dare penetrate. The curtain came down on the glorious finale. Wave upon wave of applause broke over the theatre ... But that wasn't the night's final finale!

A full hour later when the hubbub had died down and the visitors and admirers had quit back-stage, Clive waited for Siri. She was just saying good night to Rosalind Vaughan and her husband. He watched her come up to him, her lovely face glowing.

'I shouldn't be too long, Clive. Wait for me in the car if you like. It's much too cold here.'

'All right, then, I'll bring the car round to the front and meet you there in a few moments. Shall I take your case?'

'Oh yes, please!' Siri looked over her shoulder and saw it standing near the dressing rooms.

'I'll get it.' Clive moved over and picked up the case. 'Be seeing you.' He smiled and made for the stage door. Siri waited a few more minutes, then decided to go in search of St. Clair to congratulate him. He had been with the Baroness's party. She crossed over the stage and walked along to the diva's dressing room. One or two people were still chatting at the far end of the corridor. The diva's door was slightly ajar, but not a sound issued from within. It was unlike St. Clair to have left so early.

Siri peered inside for a second and froze for her trouble. The Baroness's great tawny head was thrown back to St. Clair's as his mouth came down on her own. Never before in Siri's young life had it happened to her—the sensation of something snapping in her head. Her vision became clouded and suffused with red. If only she had Brunnhilde's spear she could use it to some effect! She would run it through him, the wanton seducer flitting carefree as the honey-bee from flower to flower.

She moved away blindly, but not before Damian lifted his head and caught sight of her agonised profile. With great presence of mind he murmured something appropriate to the Baroness and followed in close pursuit. He caught her up easily, for she was not looking where she was going. She struggled against his cruel grip, but he hauled her back into one of the deserted dressing rooms, locking the door at the same time.

Her hands continued to struggle wildly in his, colour flooding her face at her own helplessness.

'Fancy meeting you here, Miss Linton,' he drawled, a little amused and totally unembarrassed.

'Lothario!' she flung at him with withering scorn, for his excesses.

'As you say, Miss Prunes,' he answered lightly, 'though I can't for the life of me see anything desperate in the situation.'

'How the devil could you after a lifetime of it?' Siri almost shouted at him, her temper making her feel quite faint. Her stormy eyes flashed over his dark, handsome face, the wickedly sardonic mouth.

He moved his hands to her shoulders, holding her still by force. 'I'm totally unused to explaining myself, but I just might on this particular occasion.' He held her fast against her struggles. 'Will you listen!'

Their eyes clashed; his a shade dangerous, hers glittering like ice crystals.

'Do you really think we have anything to say to one another?' she asked with fiery insolence.

'Volumes!' he said, hard and deliberate, 'seeing you're not sufficiently sophisticated to place the correct interpretation on my actions.'

'*Du lieber Gott!*' she muttered with the tongue of the enemy.

Even now his voice held a thread of mockery. 'The Baroness is, as you are well aware, my child, a woman of considerable consequence. She had just given a sterling performance under my direction and she does not find me unattractive. At the precise moment you happened to be poking your nose in where it was not wanted, she required me to kiss her. It's as simple as that. Perhaps you could tell me? What would you have had me do? It would have been churlish, not to say impossible, to have refused what meant absolutely nothing to me.' His tone lightened. 'I can't slight my prima donnas, you know, especially when they are of the eminence of the Baroness. Put it down to a moment's homage, if you like, though I really don't see why I should be defending myself against an inopportune child. The Baroness was elated and in a kissing mood, I suppose. I've struck any number of those occasions. This time I just happened to be handy.'

Her head came up proudly. 'Yes, of course,' she said sweetly. 'I quite see the way of it, none better. After all, I've been *handy* enough in the past. Now, would you mind unlocking that door? Clive is waiting for me.'

He clicked his tongue in intense irritation. 'I have to, just *have* to, go on to a reception. Otherwise I might do something I'd forever regret.' He unlocked the door, leading out on to the empty passageway. 'You're not a woman at all,' he accused her mercilessly. 'Just a hysterical teenager!'

'Oh, quite!' she managed, and stalked past him without another word.

Clive was waiting for her, making no mention of the time she had kept him waiting. He held the door for her and Siri slipped wordlessly into the front seat. Clive was full of the evening's performance, going on to contrast the three great schools of opera—Italian, French, German. 'It absolutely ravishes the senses, don't you think?'

'Yes, of course,' Siri answered vaguely, her thoughts in a torment. "Hysterical teenager!" he had called her, when he had aroused her womanhood!

'I'd say it was largely a matter of temperament.' Clive glanced at Siri's intent profile, but she seemed flatteringly preoccupied with his last hypothesis.

He warmed to his subject. 'Yet at times I suppose you could say a little *too* calculated!' He flung her a sweet, sideways smile—'But arguments aside, I thought the Baroness was superb! Such a fine big woman—and that voice! The power! I'll bet they could hear her for blocks.'

Siri's agitation was growing, unnoticed by Clive. Like most men nothing gave him greater pleasure than to expound his ideas to a beautiful, receptive woman.

He talked on for a few moments about Damian's masterly conception among other things, while Siri sat surrounded by her own private circle of flames. '*Abject rejection*'—the self-chosen words beat into her brain, while she held herself in check until she could reach the privacy of her own bedroom. 'There I'll break into a frenzy.'

'Did you say something?' Clive turned to her with the query.

'No, Clive, you were saying?'

'Yes, well, I wouldn't go quite so far as to say an organ-grinder's monkey.' Clive picked up where he left off.

Did all women infatuate him? My pride is wounded to the quick, Siri thought, biting hard on her full underlip. 'Ha!' she cried out in uncontrollable rage, unconsciously answering Clive.

'I knew you'd agree with me,' he said, well satisfied.

Siri gazed out at the flying miles. No moon tonight, just a handful of stars. She swallowed on the lump in her throat. Let no one be witness to her humiliation.

Clive, carried away by his own eloquence and the proximity of his darling acquiescent Siri, got on to the subject of taking up his piano scholarship in London. Siri was unusually quiet, giving him all her attention. He couldn't ever remember getting such a clear go. In the course of his monologue, emboldened by her slight air of enthralment, Clive asked her to consider, if only for a moment, joining him there. To let him smooth the way for her. Look after her on a permanent basis. Immediately he had said it, overcome by the enormity of his suggestion, Clive groaned aloud.

Siri looked at him, startled out of her thoughts of jealousy and vengeance. 'But I agree.'

The car swerved violently. 'You do?' Clive sounded incredulous.

'Yes, of course I do.' Siri strove to show a little more interest. But really, to listen to Clive's dissertations tonight of all nights was beyond her.

Clive was ecstatic. To be singled out for the love of Siri! So his mother had been right, after all, and she did care for him. His moment over, Clive fell into silence overwhelmed with a joy too deep for utterance.

Siri too was silent. She must have been unspeakably moved. At the front of the house, Clive handed her out and walked her to the door, stooping to kiss her cheek solemnly. A broken sigh escaped her.

'I shall never forget tonight,' Clive said, his sensitive face transfigured by love. But Siri was not looking at him, dominated by her need for solitude, if indeed she would have noticed anything out of the ordinary if she had.

'Neither shall I,' she added vibrantly, thrilling Clive to high heaven. 'Good night, Clive dear. Thank you so much.' She reached up and patted his cheek, leaving him with only the scent of her in the crisp night air.

Clive walked down the path. How wonderfully demure she was, he thought. 'Thank you so much'

—he was thinking of her words. How many girls of today would have thought of that? Just to think that she should thank him, when she was raising him to the stars! Just an added touch of womanliness.

He drove home, glorying in wholly requited love, leaving Siri to toss and turn and have nightmares centred around one word 'rejection'. But at least she was mercifully oblivious of her impending engagement.

Charlotte was an inveterate early riser, up and about, throwing breadcrumbs to the brazen invaders at the back door, out in the garden if it was fine and sketching if the weather wasn't obliging.

This morning, however, she just stood looking out at the bare frangipani, the tawny green winter grass crested with frost, wondering what had gone wrong with Siri's evening. She herself had gone on to a supper party with friends, returning home after midnight to find Siri in bed and feigning sleep. Of that she was certain. Charlotte had been instantly aware, as we sometimes are without quite knowing why, that her niece was upset or disturbed, or both. She had called a soft good night, allowing Siri to tell her all about it in her own time.

Charlotte stood splashing the already spotless tiles, then went about setting the table for breakfast. When things were under way she went to the bottom of the stairs and called that it was nearly half-past seven and the coffee was almost ready.

Five minutes later, Siri came padding down the stairs in her white quilted dressing gown, her thick plait over her shoulder. There was nothing of the usual impetuous rush about her descent. Charlotte smiled at her and touched her arm, putting her breakfast before her. Siri gazed down at her scrambled eggs, feeling the tears start to her eyes at such kindness taken for granted. With Charlotte, there had never been the need to develop a protective armour of silence. Charlotte never pried, never questioned. They shared one another's pleasures and disappointments voluntarily, each with an eye for the other's happiness. They had a close and understanding relationship, able to respect the other's occasional reticences.

'What is it, my darling? I just felt in my bones something was wrong.'

Charlotte watched a great tear, diamond-bright, slide down Siri's cheek, to be followed by another of equal brilliance. She made a sound of dismay and started to pour the coffee. She believed that a hot drink always helped.

'I still don't believe it,' Siri said huskily.

'Tut!' Charlotte's tongue clicked against her teeth, but otherwise she didn't interrupt the narrative.

'He kissed her, you know. I saw them. Quite unintentional—the seeing, I mean, not the kissing. I thought there might have been ...' Siri choked on her story, her eyes shadowed.

Charlotte put down her cup with a muffled exclamation. That was damned hot!

'Damian kissed the Baroness, is that it?'

'Why, yes. How did you know?'

Even under the tragic circumstances, Charlotte laughed. 'Come now, darling, you'll have to fill me in a little more completely. Damian kissed the Baroness. Is there anything more to add to it?'

Siri was speechless. 'Isn't that enough?'

'Not for me, pet. I imagine it was just one of those things.'

'Lottie!' Her niece looked over at her, openly scandalised. 'Do you mean to tell me you condone it?' Her tone was heated and passionately indignant.

Charlotte looked reflective. 'You know, my darling, in some ways you're quite unsophisticated.' She caught Siri's expression and held up her hand. 'No, let me finish. You've never been through the usual romantic skirmishes. Your sights have been solely directed towards developing your gift, with always one thing in mind. Whether Damian kissed the Baroness or not is of no great consequence. Remember, my child, he's committed to no one, a free agent, and he has been for a long time. He can kiss any woman he pleases, within a reasonable limit.'

Siri interrupted. 'He said it would have been churlish to have refused. Terribly obliging, isn't he? Next they'll be stopping him in the streets. He said she was expecting to be kissed and that was that. A gentleman could hardly refuse. The mind boggles! He called it a kind of homage.'

Charlotte threw up her hands. 'Well, there you

are, love. Damian goes his own way, answerable to no one, so what are you looking so tragic for?'

'But really, Lottie!'

'Do see it in perspective, dear,' Charlotte warned. 'Damian is a man of the world, moving among highly gifted and quite extraordinary people. I should say that sort of thing happens all the time in the theatre without necessarily meaning anything.'

'Goodness, you *are* tolerant!' Siri said in as reasonable a tone as she could manage.

'Now, now, Siri, don't be childish. Without taking Damian's part I would say it happened just as he said. He may be wildly attractive to women, but he has a hard core of integrity, I'm certain of it.'

'And I'm being unbearably censorious.' Siri raised her eyes to her aunt's face.

'Just a little, darling, but I can see what a shock it must have been for you.'

'Shock?' Siri's laugh trembled. Then, surprisingly, she started in on her scrambled eggs which Charlotte had sensibly covered, followed by two pieces of toast and another cup of coffee. With the resilience of youth, breakfast was disposed of. 'You're a wonderfully calm woman, Lottie. It shines out of your face.'

Charlotte gave an appreciative laugh. 'Put it down to age and experience. It comes to us all. Now what's on the agenda for today?'

Before Charlotte's eyes, Siri had brightened into her old self. Siri was now enjoying a delicious half-muffled yawn, showing the tip of her tongue curled like a kitten's.

'Nothing much. Clive and I are due at the theatre this morning for a little coaching. Madame this afternoon, then the performance.'

'You told Damian what you thought?'

Siri coloured. 'I'm afraid so.'

'Never mind,' Charlotte said soothingly, seeing vivid colour slides of Siri's reaction to the contretemps. 'Just act as though nothing happened. I'm sure he will . . .'

It was good advice and it would have worked but for only one thing. Clive decided to announce their engagement. When Siri arrived at the theatre, the smiles from the cast seemed to her more than usually warm and welcoming. *Siegfried* was scheduled for that night. Some of the cast not present in the dramatic action of *Die Walküre* were due for reappearance. To her surprise, Clive greeted her with a kiss on the cheek. Come to think of it, Siri remembered that he had kissed her the same way the previous night. Siri wasn't sure that she wanted it repeated.

'I realise now I shouldn't have, but I've broken the news.'

What *was* Clive whispering about? 'The news?' Siri looked up at him quizzically.

A well-padded arm went round her. The contralto playing Erde gave her a friendly squeeze.

'My very warmest best wishes, Serena. Our Clive's a lucky young man and he knows it, bless him.' She smiled over at the beaming Clive.

Siri blushed deeply and seemed acutely embarrassed. My stars! How had it happened? Was she still in the middle of her nightmare? Her mind raced back over the last evening. There wasn't a single thing she could recall which could have accounted for Clive's extraordinary behaviour: Or was there? Admittedly she hadn't heard a word he said, but then she was equally certain he hadn't mentioned anything the like of this unlikely alliance.

Siri looked at him aghast. This morning he was absolutely buoyant, inspired, fresh and joyful. What could have happened to him? He had turned aside to answer one of the sopranos, a shout of laughter giving vent to his high spirits.

Erde was eyeing her speculatively. Serena was acting strangely for a newly engaged girl.

'Miss Linton, please.' Damian St. Clair appeared in the wings, withdrawing as soon as he had directed his summons.

Siri hurried up the side steps and through to his rooms.

He looked a stranger, dark and formidable. The door was firmly shut behind her. 'I'll say this for you, Siri. You give as good as you get!'

'But I don't understand a word of it!'

'Obviously!' His dark eyes raked her face. 'You're no one's idea of a radiant bride-to-be. But tell me, why take your temper out on that unfortunate young man?'

'Well, he for one looks quite pleased with himself,' she was stung into mentioning.

He laughed, a harsh, sardonic sound. 'Give him time! Or rather, give *you* time. However he came to love such a capricious beauty, I can't imagine. You're a horrible, horrible little girl!'

Her eyes were deeply shadowed, as if she hadn't slept very well. She looked back at him, her soft, sensuous mouth parting with contrition. 'I can't explain how it happened, Damian. Please believe me.'

'Did you believe *me*?' he cut her off ruthlessly, in an extreme temper. 'And now you must pay the price, you infuriating, time-consuming, mindless little idiot!'

Siri fell back at his dark fury. 'You don't care at all,' she accused him. 'You don't, do you? You heartless creature! You're just using me.'

He made a lunge for her, bringing her hard up against him. 'Don't tremble, you little fool!' he muttered darkly.

A knock at the door brought them sharply apart. Siri moved like a startled fawn, taking a chair at the far side of the executive desk which had been provided for Damian's use. The whole thing was fantastic!

Hector Mainwaring stood on the threshold somewhat hesitantly for him. 'Morning, St. Clair.' His eyes went beyond the conductor, seeing Serena. 'Ah, the cruel Miss Linton! How could you lead us on so?' He came into the room without further invitation, taking Siri's hand. 'And I could have loved you to distraction.'

'You're still at liberty to do so,' Siri said a trifle wildly. She fled from the room, leaving the bass gazing after her in puzzled wonderment.

It wasn't until lunch time that Siri had an opportunity for private conversation with her fiancé. She had suggested coffee at the Milano and Clive had only been too pleased to fall in with the idea. The restaurant was blissfully quiet after the hubbub of the theatre.

Clive was watching her draw off her gloves with all the fascination of a man at the unveiling of a small masterpiece. 'I love you in that dress,' he said endearingly. His compliment was even more endearing because the dress was a recent unworn purchase.

'Clive dear.'

'Yes, my love?'

So soon to fall into character? Siri tried again. 'Clive, I must speak to you.'

'You've thought better of it. Is that what you're trying to tell me?'

'Not exactly.' Her smoky eyes were clouded with concern. 'You see, Clive, I was upset about something last night and preoccupied with it and I just failed to grasp what you were saying to me. It was unforgivable, I know.'

'Holy hell!' The words were torn from him.

'I'm afraid so, Clive. What did you say to me?'

Clive was clutching desperately at the tablecloth.

'Careful, you'll tip the coffee!' Siri hastily shifted the cup and saucer to a safer position.

'Well, there's no point in saying it now as you weren't interested then. I did ask you to let me look after you on a permanent basis.'

'*Grand Dio!*'

'Exactly. What a fool I've been. Even Mother was flabbergasted. I say, Siri, I've made an absolute ass of you too.' Even in the face of his own misery Clive's thoughts were of Siri's embarrassment.

'It's my own fault, Clive. I should have been paying attention, I always do, strangely enough. It was just last night—being upset, you see. Please forgive me.'

He covered her hand with his own, looking off into space.

'Drink your coffee, Clive. Mine's cold.'

'You don't love me, Siri. How could I have thought otherwise? Diana and the shepherd boy.'

Siri smiled at the extravagant simile. 'But I *do* love you, Clive, and I respect our friendship. It's just that I'm not *in* love with you. You do see the difference.'

'Oh, I see all right. But what am I to do? Everyone will know by now, rash idiot that I am.'

Her smooth brow puckered. 'We'll simply have to stay engaged until the end of the season. Then we can break it off discreetly. I won't have you exposed to ridicule.'

'I say, that's going a bit far for me, Siri. I don't deserve it.'

'Well, I can't think of anything else. Can you? The harm's done. Oh dear! You know what I mean.'

Clive had visibly flinched. 'You don't love me,' he murmured dejectedly.

'You're upsetting me, Clive. I'm so sorry to have

119

misled you like this. I do love you, like a dear cousin perhaps.'

'Yes, yes—ah well! I think I'll stay a bachelor after all.'

'Perhaps it might be for the best, for the time being anyway, Clive. You have so much to accomplish—your scholarship, your accompanying. You can't afford to be thinking of marriage yet.'

He smiled without bitterness. 'You've talked me out of it, Siri. Now let me get this straight. We're engaged until the end of the season, is that it?'

'Yes. You can depend on me to back you up.'

'It strikes me this conversation is ridiculous. Are you sure it's what you want?'

'I can't say it's what I want, Clive, but it's the best we can do under the circumstances.'

'You may even get to like it.' Clive almost brightened.

Siri started. 'I can't allow you to think or hope along those lines, Clive. Now or ever, I'm sorry.' She sounded distressed.

'I was only joking anyway.' He put a brave face on it and pocketed the change. 'Now if you're ready I'll walk you down to the studio? ...'

But it was not as easy as all that. Madame Castelli had to be told. It would have been unthinkable to allow her to hear the news second-hand. Siri debated whether to tell her the whole truth or what passed for the truth. In the end she decided on the latter. Madame was constitutionally incapable of keeping a secret, unless it was her age, or what became of her husband. But she did react like a dragon.

'So—' she screeched. 'Not the singer already and you think of the marriage. Next the *bambinos*. Pouf!'

'But surely, Madame, you would expect me to marry eventually.' The black eyes were indignant.

'I am human. I know what to expect, but not the young Martyn. He is not for you. Today you make me feel old and depressed.' She looked speculative, her eyes brightening. 'Need you marry him?' Madame was not always consistent.

'We hadn't gone so far ahead. We're only just engaged.'

The knot on top of Madame's head began to shake and shake again. 'I'm in pain, I'm sure it is pain. You have a great voice, Serena *cara*, I can tell you, you are not stupid or vain, but no future with that young man. Only one other can I think of to guard you and your voice.'

She almost evoked a response, but Siri decided to stick to her predetermined course, feigning perplexity.

'Shall we go over Act II of *Traviata*, Madame?'

'As you please, child.' Just so had she complicated her own girlhood. Giorgio had not died, never weep for him! He had deserted her, one year after Tonio had been born. *Libertino!* Going off with a second-rate mezzo-soprano. 'Zut!' she cried aloud.

'Come, child, Violetta awaits our attention,' she said grimly.

Siri put the score in front of her teacher. Madame ran a distracted hand through her coiffure. It now stood up in a crest like some exotic bird. There was a hectic flush of colour in her olive cheeks that made Siri feel guilty. She had been purposely vague about her engagement, fearing Madame's knowing eye and runaway tongue. According to Castelli, great voices did not belong to their owners, but rather to the world. Now Clive Martyn was threatening that world. Siri knew a momentary weakening. She was very fond of Castelli. Madame was thumbing through the well-worn score with an abstracted air. Suddenly Siri longed for Charlotte, for her tranquillity, her fine integrity. Someone close to her to share this unexpected turmoil.

Madame's voice startled her out of her preoccupation. 'From the beginning, *cara*. . . . *E strano*. . . .'

Siri began to sing and the peaked, strained look began to die out of Castelli's face. It was replaced by a ripple of approval, then another, then a longer one. Such a voice! She had heard no other quite like it. That curious sensuous lushness, full of mystery and splendour, almost like a mezzo with a phenomenal range. Madame listened intently, her ear and judgment impeccable. Oh, that she would live to hear the child at the peak of her accomplishment. That would be really something!

By the end of the day, Siri's own state of mind had grown correspondingly restless and anxious. Clive was waiting for her after the lesson, but mercifully out in the street.

They planned to tell Charlotte together, but when they drove up to the front of the house Charlotte was standing in intent conversation with

Damian, the front gate swinging gently backwards and forwards in the breeze. Siri couldn't look at either of them, cursing herself, and by this time Clive as well, for the fool position they were in.

'Am I to understand congratulations are in order?' St. Clair inquired with a supercilious lift of his fine black brows.

Clive coloured and stammered, 'Why, yes, thank you, sir.' That St. Clair was the very devil, he thought wretchedly. He shot a glance at Siri's aunt who also wore an air of displeasure.

If looks were blows I would be down there on the pavement, Siri thought dispiritedly. His lean dark face looked impossibly forbidding. His respect was now unattainable.

'Well, come into the house, children. I imagine you have something to tell me.' Charlotte turned to her niece, who had never been more conspicuously silent.

'Yes, children, *do*,' Damian encouraged, with what seemed to Siri malicious relish. He turned back to Charlotte with obvious relief: adult to adult!

'I'll go along, Charlotte. You're coming Saturday evening, of course.

'Looking forward to it immensely.'

'Good.' Damian opened the car door and slid into the driver's seat, flickering one thunderous glance over the defenceless Siri. 'Goodbye, Martyn.' He nodded curtly to Clive, who was in an agony of embarrassment.

All three of them watched the car disappear over

the brow of the hill, then with one accord they started back to the house.

Charlotte decided on diplomacy. 'You speak first, Siri. I've purposely kept my mind a blank in case you decided to tell me.'

Siri breathed deeply. 'The fact is, Lottie. . . .' she began, and launched into her tale.

Charlotte gazed from one to the other in astonishment. 'So you're doing this to avoid gossip?'

'Why, yes,' Clive said rapidly.

Charlotte got up and took a quick turn around the room. 'I think I'll have a gin and tonic. What about you two? I guess you need it.'

'A beer would do just as well,' Clive answered despondently.

'I didn't know you drank at all, Clive.' Siri looked taken aback for a moment.

'I'm about due to start. Honestly, Miss Frampton, I can't say how sorry I am.'

'Thank you, Clive,' Charlotte said dryly. 'Siri's consideration is equally magnanimous. Quite noble, in fact.'

Siri stood up with a quick determined movement. 'I won't have Clive made fun of. It's only for a short time and no harm done. I'll come out to the car with you, Clive,' she said hastily.

Charlotte looked ready to explode.

When Siri came back, her aunt had started on her second gin. 'But you're ready to make a fool of yourself.'

'Oh, please, Lottie. I have a splitting headache. What did Damian want?'

'To stop it, child. What else? You can imagine how stunned I was.'

'He looked furious.'

'He was and is. Come to think of it, he's a man to be feared. Ah, well, you young people will have to work it out for yourselves. One never gets thanked for interfering.'

'I'm so sorry, Lottie,' Siri said, after a moment's silence.

'You silly child.' Charlotte's voice was the same, calm and loving. 'Come along now and we'll start tea, otherwise we'll run ourselves late for this evening.'

She got to her feet, passing her hand lightly and lovingly over Siri's shoulder, and then there was peace between them.

CHAPTER TEN

SATURDAY morning Charlotte and Siri drove into the city to have their hair done at Stefan's. Steffi, as he was called by the staff, was 'the' hairdresser and a stranger to them both.

Charlotte had been up for hours, working in a sheltered part of the garden, sinking an old bath to half its depth in the ground, the basis for her planned corner pool and rockery. Goldfish were envisaged, as well perhaps as some gorgeous water-lilies, and everywhere and all over there would be sprouting greenery. She had already selected the flat rocks to face the bath, and placed them in a tidy heap ready for cementing. The chicken wire, too, had come off the bulb garden. The long granite outcrop guarding the front of the house had been crying out for the softening influence of flowers. She could hardly wait for the anticipated sea of colour washing the grey neutrality of the rocks. There were scillas and tulips, daffodils and hya-cinths and, in the centre, big creamy White Emper-ors, all set down in a drifting pattern. Charlotte preferred interlocking grouping rather than the set blobs of colour which Hettie Lawrence had tried to talk her in to. Her autumnal expense and effort seemed to be paying dividends. All of the plants were flourishing, even the miniature hya-cinths she had set in the cracks and crevices of the rock face, ready-made plant pockets. With the sweet flush of spring, her twenty-foot crescent, her once ugly duckling, would be transformed into a dazzling swan.

So immersed was she that Siri had to call not once, but three times before Charlotte came in. Even so, they arrived at the salon before time. It was terribly stylish, and so was Steffi, tall and elegant with luxuriant golden whiskers and very forthright opinions.

'Too dreadful, my dear!' He gave a small shriek and gave orders to change the shade of Charlotte's usual tint job. He was 'definitely against it, and quite frankly for' what he specifically suggested— Brownette No. 23.

Then it was Siri's turn, and nothing else would do but to take several inches off her hair, thus allowing her to wear it up or down as the mood took her.

As it was, Steffi was shocked by her timidity. 'Women come to me begging to be made beautiful, and here you are, a true beauty, failing in your God-given duty.'

Obviously a woman's main function, or one of them, was to gladden the eye. As he spoke, Steffi uncoiled her heavy loop of hair, reparting it dead centre, and drawing it back over her shoulders, all the while gazing into the mirror in the manner of a fairy godmother. 'See how the eyes shine out. Such perfect symmetry! Such bone structure! We must draw the fullest attention to it.' His eyes met hers hypnotically. 'I feel exhilarated. Yes, exhilarated, I tell you.'

Siri felt her teeth tighten in some trepidation. 'How much do you intend to take off?'

Steffi snapped the scissors with a practised, determined hand. 'Oh, don't be an old maid. Where's your bezazz! I promise you will look like a goddess on a pedestal. The Goddess of Love!' he breathed with almost feminine detachment.

The scissors flew, the locks fell, but not drastically. When he finally stepped back after thinning and shaping, Siri's hair still hung a good few inches over her shoulders.

Steffi snapped his fingers in the air, and immediately an assistant was beside him. 'Body and movement,' he announced dogmatically. His command was taken up by the dandified young man just starting sideburns. The latter really intrigued Siri, smiling shyly every time their eyes met in the mirror. She hated having her hair washed and washed, then rinsed repeatedly, and just as she thought it all over, rinsed again. But Steffi himself combed it out, parted in the centre, raised on the crown and swinging in a lengthening curve over her shoulders. It was a style that demanded youth and beautiful features, but, if you had them, the effect was sensational. Now more than ever she looked the romantic heroine of fiction.

'You admit I was right?' Steffi had his head on one side, transfixing her gaze.

'Why, yes, it's wonderfully flattering.' —And uncomfortable, Siri amended inwardly, completely unused to having her hair swinging free. The impulse to tie it all back would undoubtedly get the better of her.

'Flattery, bah!' Steffi was disdainful. 'You have no need of flattery. The style *is* you. No, don't touch it. I can see it feels strange to you.'

Siri smiled at him, her eyes luminous with pleasure and amusement. 'Need I say I'll come to no other?'

Steffi was unmoved. 'Of course.—And now your lady mother.'

Siri looked around wildly. *Her lady mother!* Her Aunt Charlotte looked wonderful. The new shade was a soft natural mid-brown with no trace of the reddish-gold tinge they were used to from Renata's. It was difficult to say why it made such a difference. It just did. Of course, the set was softer, more off the face, with the all-important look of individuality. Steffi had no use for carbon-copy clients. He strongly advocated the 'you' look, only more so.

Charlotte looked very pleased with herself and spoke most graciously to Steffi as she booked another appointment for a month ahead. Under Steffi's stern eye Siri felt obliged to do the same. Out in the street she broke into laughter.

'That style *is* you, my lady mother.'

'Gracious, is that what he called me?' Charlotte stopped dead to look at her.

'Yes, though the expression and not the idea is what's making me laugh. He's quite a character, don't you think?'

Charlotte patted her set serenely. 'Well, I for one approve of him. I feel amazingly confident, ready for anything.'

And to prove it she took Siri's arm, drawing her into an expensive boutique.

It was unanimously agreed by the Press and public alike that the German diva reached her greatest heights in *Gotterdammerung*. Her characterisation had been extremely effective, backed by her magnificent stage presence. If it were possible, the theatre was even more packed on the Saturday than the opening night, and the feminine display of affluence during the intervals was simply staggering! The society writers had a gushingly good time.

Siri and Charlotte, knowing what to expect, had taken great pains with their dressing. Siri wore a flaring floor-length shift of French grey velvet, the tiny slip top a torrent of brilliants, crystal dewdrops and flowers of silver with a matching jewelled bolero, while Charlotte had completely let her head go for a model gown of pimpernel red silk handsomely embroidered with Portuguese braid. Her fur was far from new, but it still looked good.

The talk and the laughter in the foyer bespoke the audience's enjoyment. Through the four nights, they had been absorbed into an imaginary epoch, lived the lives of gods and demi-gods, mythological figures so vividly drawn as to be historical. Under Damian St. Clair's direction, all unduly prolonged scenes, unnecessary to the development of the plot, had been deleted. Nothing extraneous had been allowed to detract from the over-all sublimity of the score. The mounting had been superb. Those who had ventured out on the social scene, equally disposed to be bored or to applaud, found themselves left with their palms tingling. Damian St. Clair had shown himself not only a man of considerable artistic stature, but an operatic director with a rare understanding of singers.

The curtain came down and the applause was deafening. The Baroness received no less than ten curtain calls, all studies in elaborate byplay and professional graciousness. The front of the stage was covered with flowers as she bent and picked up one perfect rose, handing it across the footlights to the conductor. Her sincerity and great artistry caused the applause to break out afresh, bringing Damian on to the stage. To explosive volleys of appreciation he took the diva's outstretched hand and kissed it in the grand manner.

The Baroness looked transfigured, radiant with her reception. But she was not to relax. A celebration party had been arranged at the Darling Point mansion of Charles Morgenstern, the Australian manager of Carola Records, the diva's recording company. It was due to last well into the small hours.

The Morgensterns' was one of the few large estates left in the Metropolitan area. It covered roughly four acres, kept a gardener full time, and was the perfect setting for the one-hundred-and-ten-year-old-mansion of sandstone and white cast-iron lace, an immensely charming legacy of the past.

The massive front gates stood open to the wide-gravelled driveway flanked by poplars and dominated by an enormous pin oak at the end of the drive. Siri drove slowly, ignoring the headlights in her rear vision. Cars were parked four deep at all stages of the drive and out in the quiet and exclusive cul-de-sac. Broad beams of rose and gold streamed from both stories of the house, flooding the terrace with an expansive party-loving atmosphere. Most of the guests had assembled by the time Siri and Charlotte parked the car and found their way to the reception hall.

A pendant chandelier straight out of a fairy tale lit the space with a myriad reflections and caught its own loveliness in the large elaborately framed mirror hanging above a Buhl cabinet. Their hostess, a charming and highly intelligent lady, was on hand to greet them, drawing them into the main throng.

Siri and Charlotte looked round them with pleasure, openly admiring such an extraordinarily happy marriage of colonial elegance and the spirited contemporary style. As they moved into the lofty corniced living room, with its elaborate frieze-work and fluted columns, spaces seemed to expand on one another, emphasizing the feeling of grandeur. In actual fact, the partition dividing the handsome double parlours had been removed soon after the Morgensterns had moved into their then rather neglected mansion. Money, effort, and productive minds had done the rest.

Long elegant buffet tables covered with ice-pink

linen a foot deep in lace, had been set to work in tandem. One sparkled with crystals and every alcoholic beverage one could think of, and the other gleamed with silver and quite beautiful china. Masses of camellias were arranged in huge goblets with slender tapers crisscrossed between the pink and white of the exquisite blossoms. It was a beautiful, festive scene, quite fitting the occasion. The room was possibly the most beautiful they had ever been in. It was almost asymmetrical, with floor to ceiling glass panels overlooking the park-like gardens. And if you got tired of the view, there were treasures galore in the room behind you.

Siri looked over her shoulder at Charlotte. She was smiling slightly, gazing out at the floodlight terrace, seeing in her mind's eye the splendours of the blue-black garden beyond it. The house and the terrace were thronged with people, but not uncomfortably so. It was a mansion, after all. There were singers, actors, writers, artists and, unless Siri was very much mistaken, that was the German Ambassador.

Out on the terrace a leading trio was playing, while couples danced, or more accurately circled one another with a return to propriety. At least two of them were drawing attention to themselves with their vivacity and abandon. Further down the garden and around the enormous aquamarine pool were black silhouettes of heads and shoulders, never anything else but *à deux*.

Siri stood in the centre of the beautiful crimson carpet and gazed around with a fascinated eye. Two slender, languid young men in jewel-coloured Nehru jackets were talking at once with bantering inconsequence. They were, and were accepted as, quite gifted oddities, while a very statuesque red-head was standing with her head thrown back at the reflected gold of the French windows, her white dress rippling and fluttering as if she were about to take flight.

Charlotte had been caught up by a lethargic lady wearing a quantity of diamonds who proclaimed herself familiar with Charlotte's work as an illustrator. The lady looked lethargic, but was in fact a highly successful business woman. Her contrived ennui, adopted in the early days to fool her competitors, had become habitual but just as deceptive.

At the far side of the room the well-known radio personality, Gertie Howard, was holding forth to a small group, her heavy, pleasantly ugly face brimming alive to her own conversational monologue. Some of those around her secretly nourished the hope that she would put her stole in it, but felt obliged to look vivid, lest their heads roll on one of her programmes. 'Of course, darlings, before I go on I stand alone in that awful grey world, almost like the confessional.'

'Oh, surely not,' a rash young man in garnet trousers burst out. Miss Howard turned her back on him and gave her full attention to Dr Robert Greenwood, the noted music critic, whose excessively high forehead gave him the traditional look of genius. It was an entirely erroneous impression, but it served its purpose. There were many in the city who never knew if they had witnessed a triumph or a débâcle until they had read Dr. Greenwood's column.

Siri moved over to a wing-backed chair covered in strawberry velvet, catching every male eye in the group near her.

'—— reads books with terribly long words in them,' an aggressively stout old lady was insisting. 'I never said scientific,' she burst out laughing. Her face, above her violet gown, contained the violent innuendoes of a lifetime. As she laughed, clusters of amethysts swung madly from her ears. Laughter broke out among the others infecting those at the bar, which was not yet in full swing. At the opposite end of the room a slight young man was playing the piano and beside him stood a plump and pretty Jewish lady engaged in singing jazz. She sang it rather badly but had drunk too much champagne to tell the difference. At her husband's suggestion that she sing a little opera, she fell back against the keyboard with a small shriek and a discordant clatter.

'They don't write tunes like that any more,' Jon Lawnton breathed in her ear with enormous relish.

Siri smiled, looking up at him. 'The wicked Mr. Lawnton.'

'My pleasure, darling.' He drew up a chair near her. 'And where is the fiancé, dear child?'

Siri started. Was there any snippet of gossip he missed? 'A previous engagement,' she lied with mild resentment.

He smiled knowledgeably and settled back in his

chair, accepting another Martini from a remarkably unobtrusive host. Siri had graciously declined. She had no intention of becoming talkative with Jon Lawnton.

'Extraordinarily beautiful room, isn't it? Natalie has a positive genius for collecting lovely objects.'

'Surely it wouldn't be too difficult with the right amount of money.'

'You'd be surprised, child.' He leaned forward and, in a confidential murmur, proceeded to reduce to a barn the sixty-thousand-dollar retreat of two of his dearest friends. He broke off with a muffled groan. 'Don't look now, but that fearful bore, Gertie Howard, is coming towards us. Her success would seem to indicate corruption in high places. What say we dance?'

They were too late. Gertie Howard, guessing their intention, had put on an impressive turn of speed. 'Jonathan darling——' She flung out her arms, gathering the wholly responsive Lawnton to her.

'Gertie sweetie, I was hoping to see you tonight.' He kissed her resoundingly, turning her towards Siri. 'Darling, I don't think you know Miss Linton?'

'Of course I do. It's my business, remember?' She grasped Siri's hand with bone-cracking ferocity. 'Catherine Frampton's daughter, if you were blind enough to miss it. I was one of the first to write up your mother. Did you know that, child?'

Siri looked serious. 'No, I didn't, Miss Howard.'

'Yes, indeed.' The other woman was running a

hawk-eye over her. 'Got a great voice, I hear. I'd like to be the judge of that. Perhaps later.'

The pleasure of the evening started to wane. The first stone in the tranquil pond. 'I don't think so, Miss Howard. It wouldn't be exactly the appropriate time.'

'Hum. We'll see.' She swivelled all of a sudden, her fabled senses alerted. The guests of honour had that instant arrived, surrounded by a beaming circle of admirers. Somehow the svelte redhead was holding on to Damian's arm, her head thrown back in the attitude she had been practising.

Siri failed to notice. She had her sights set on St. Clair. She heard no music, saw no one. Ribbons of laughter trailed over her head. There was only his handsome dark head, his eyes scanning the room. Quickly she turned her head as his gaze slid over her. Her dark hair, the pallor of her lovely skin, shone across the room, her serenity a mask, something unreal. She could feel her heart thudding. For an instant everything was driven from her mind, her surroundings fading in the mist of swirling senses.

It was always there: the longing to see him. Deliberately he turned his dark head, seeking out the attention of his hostess. Siri bit her lip, feeling his bitter rejection. And now the party got into full swing. Everyone seemed to be talking and laughing at once.

Siri was sealed in a prison of loneliness. Except for the times she knew his eyes were upon her, those times when her heart throbbed with a dull excitement, Damian had not come near her. To everyone else, she seemed both gay and beautiful. Not for anything would she wear her heart on her sleeve. Several people who had been present at the Viscontis' had expressed their desire to hear her sing, and even as they spoke to her, Siri could feel hostility lurking across the room.

The Signora's scarlet gown was sumptuously beautiful, but there was a high colour in her cheeks, a restless glitter to her artificial gaiety, giving the impression that she was strung up on wires. Siri determined to steer clear of the Signora. Santegelo had developed one of her hates.

A discussion on the physical signposts of history: paintings versus literature, versus architecture, etc., was just starting to get pleasantly heated when Siri drifted down to the piano. Most of the guests were at the other end of the room or out on the terrace. She sat down on the brocade-covered bench, experiencing the never-diminishing thrill of the smooth ivory under her fingertips.

The exquisite romanticism of a Liszt Consolation stole into the room. St. Clair came in from the terrace, irresistibly drawn by the music. He stood beside her for a moment, then his right hand picked up the melody in an unbroken movement. Siri moved, letting him finish. He was worlds removed from her as a pianist. No one in the room came near them, sensitive to his splendid isolation.

Siri watched the long, beautiful hands on the keyboard. After a moment he lifted his head, directly meeting her liquid grey eyes.

'How unreal your composure, Siri. Or are you weaving a spell?' His voice and his nearness turned reality and order upside down for her. The room spun round. Only he was constant.

'I love you,' she said without even knowing she had said it aloud.

His hand closed over hers, meaning to, and succeeding in hurting her. 'You tell me *now*. In a room full of people, when there's no way of proving or disproving it. I'll make you pay for that.'

She shivered, reacting under compulsion to his physical presence. He seemed more angry than pleased with her involuntary declaration. She cursed her stupidity, her runaway tongue.

'I tell you, if I were young Martyn I'd hot-foot it over here *prestissimo*.' Hector Mainwaring loomed up beside them, his eyes bright and innocent as an angel's treading where angels would fear to tread.

'My head is quite clear on all points,' St. Clair pointed out, quite mildly for him.

'Well, you've a better head than I have, old son. I find Miss Linton absolutely intoxicating. Especially with the new hairdo.' His amber eyes caressed the soft skin, the swirling jet of her hair.

St. Clair got to his feet, his dark face sombre.

'I say, don't leave me,' Mainwaring remonstrated. 'There's an amorous widow over there been telling me she must be abnormal.'

'Really?' Siri asked, laughing.

'Yes, really.' He turned to look earnestly at her. 'It seems she prefers *men* to *women*!'

'Then she's one hundred per cent normal.' St.

139

Clair drawled. 'Most women *do*!'

The widow advanced with a very normal reaction to an attractive man, so far as Siri could see.

Mainwaring fled, hissing at Siri, 'Don't forget, I would die for you.'

Siri looked fleetingly into Damian's eyes, insensate to the whirl of colour around her.

'Maestro!' Santegelo swept up with her customary imperious air. Her flashing eyes dismissed Siri.

'Excuse me, won't you,' Siri murmured satirically.

The Signora had consented to sing under pressure, if someone would accompany her. No, definitely *not* Miss Linton. *Non posso*! Dr. Greenwood agreed to do the honours, seeing St. Clair was making no move to do so. Fortunately it was Musetta's Waltz Song, a simple accompaniment that would do no harm to his reputation.

The room hushed like magic while the diva settled into the curve of the grand. In a way the aria was very polished, very appealing, Siri decided. It was an open secret that the Italian diva was having trouble with the extreme notes of her range, but the high notes of the Waltz Song didn't trouble her in the least—tossed off here; beautifully sustained there.

The applause was politely enthusiastic. Something in the diva's manner had got through to them all. Perhaps they sensed the difficult period she was to go through. Her sleek dark head was bowed to their applause, one very white hand on her bosom.

Even if she did lose her voice, there were still those rubies! Weren't they marvellous! With the motion of a superbly gliding swan, the Baroness sailed through the crowd, who respectfully fell back at her approach. She stopped and kissed her colleague's smooth cheek, murmuring appreciation.

Von Richter was something of a phenomenon among prima donnas. She had no fierce competitive spirit, no 'killer instinct' and had never in her life been jealous of a rival. Her happy halo of assurance had never gone awry, but she still felt for others less fortunate. Santegelo badly needed reassurance and the Baroness was there to give it.

The two sopranos moved back into their set, the Baroness having previously declined to give a solo on the grounds that she was exhausted. No one saw fit to mention her highly contradictory face and manner.

In a far corner of the room, the unbalanced lady was ensconced on a love-seat with Hector Mainwaring. He was bearing up remarkably well, a whole tray of drinks balanced on a velvet ottoman at their feet. When asked for a song he brought the whole house down with 'Some Enchanted Evening' preceded by a very funny story about Enzio Pinza.

In her bones Siri knew she would not be allowed to escape notice. Every so often she had felt eyes upon her directed by the indefatigable Gertie Howard. Charlotte, she was surprised to note, was in the constant company of a tall distinguished man who looked vaguely familiar. Her aunt looked her very best, Siri decided.

That redhead in the white dress was being blatantly obvious. Surely Damian could see it? Her hand hovering, never quite touching his. Those eyelashes were a bit much, if it was gala! Half as much would have done twice as well.

Siri gave a start. Natalie Morgenstern was at her elbow. She was smiling and following the direction of Siri's gaze. 'We would love to hear you sing, Miss Linton. Of course, if you prefer not to, I quite understand.'

Siri's attention was caught and held by the vivid blue gaze. 'I'd be happy to repay just a little of your wonderful hospitality, Mrs Morgenstern.'

'Why, thank you, dear. Shall I announce you?'

Siri nodded her dark head and her hostess took her arm and drew her into the centre of the room.

'Ladies and gentlemen, one of our own young singers, Miss Serena Linton—some of you had the opportunity of hearing Miss Linton at the Viscontis'. Now it is our turn.'

The clapping broke out as Siri walked to the piano. Dr. Greenwood panicked for a moment. This young woman would be sure to pick something with a fearfully difficult accompaniment. His panic subsided. Damian St. Clair was beside him like a mind-reader. The doctor gave way graciously, relieved to bits! St. Clair looked up, applauding her tranquillity. She was nervous and she knew it, but she had herself under control.

Her great eyes questioned him. 'What shall it be?'

'Nothing spectacular,' he said crisply. '*Songs My Mother Taught Me* would do.'

Siri's face grew serious. The first time she had seen him, her heart had stopped beating. Now it beat with a wild insistence. His lean hands came down on the piano and the hauntingly nostalgic introduction spilled into the room, setting the mood of the song. Her voice, rounded, sensuous, intensely female, floated in the extreme quietness.

> 'Songs my mother taught me
> in the days long vanished!
> Seldom from my eyelids
> were the tear-drops banished!'

Sophisticated as they were, everyone in the room found it necessary to summon up rigid control. Such a moving quality was in the voice, the words so deeply touching, that it was almost impossible to conceal the heart's response. Involuntarily, Charlotte's hand closed on her companion's, the tears sparkling unashamedly. He patted her hand gently. The child was a revelation, of that he was certain, although he was no great authority on the voice. When the last chord had faded away the complete silence was the most perfect compliment of all. St. Clair permitted an encore, the contrast of the graceful '*Matinata*'.

The performance had taken hold of the audience. Siri found herself discovered by Dr. Greenwood and consequently bored to tears until well after supper. Santegelo waited her chance.

Siri's performance had come as a personal affront. Her explosive temperament was walking a tightrope. She would like to catapult this young woman, with her prodigious gifts, right out of the scene. Nothing came to mind. Nothing civilised, that is. There she was, insinuating herself with that Greenway person.

Dr. Greenwood paused to set down his umpteenth rum and Coca-Cola and Santegelo moved, taking up a position between the two Louis Quatorze bergères, attempting through her complete immobility to conceal her intentions. At the crucial moment she swept through the centre, tipping the small cocktail table and the entire contents of Dr. Greenwood's glass on to Siri's lap.

Siri jumped up quickly, not feeling how cold the drink was for the disfiguring stain on the velvet.

'Great Scott! I'd call that intentional.' Dr. Greenwood began mopping Siri's gown ineffectually.

'Your pardon, Signor?' Santegelo's harsh tone broke the harmony.

'I'm afraid I cannot, Madame,' he said, looking up from his task.

Siri stood transfixed until her hostess swept her up with a deft hand, shielding her with the voluminous skirt of her hostess gown.

St. Clair followed them out quickly. 'It might be best if I take you home, Siri.' Natalie offered no opposition. It was clearly what he meant to do, and he just as clearly was used to having his own way.

'But Charlotte? My coat, my purse ...' Siri was

dithering. St. Clair looked across at his hostess, making the decisions.

'I would say Charlotte is being well looked after and enjoying herself far too much to leave at the moment. Mrs. Morgenstern will see that she brings your things.' He smiled at Natalie with the full weight of his charm. She responded accordingly. He was quite the most devastating man she had ever encountered. Heaven help this gorgeous young thing if she was involved with him, she thought wryly.

She turned to Siri with marked sincerity. 'I so much enjoyed your singing, Miss Linton. Perhaps enjoyed is the wrong word. You almost reduced me to tears.'

For a moment Siri forgot her stained dress. 'That was very kind of you.'

The other woman smiled. 'Not kind, my dear, only truth! Now about your dress. . . .'

The two men walked out to the front door while St. Clair collected his coat. He was back within a minute, slipping it around Siri's shoulders.

'I'll explain the incident to your aunt,' Natalie said dryly.

None of them mentioned the fact that it was contrived.

St. Clair turned to his hostess. 'I should be back within forty minutes. By then it will be time for breakfast.'

Natalie laughed on a note of pure enjoyment. 'Don't hurry. Quite a few will still be here. *And* for breakfast. Come again, my dear,' she called to Siri over St. Clair's dark head. 'Just give me a ring and let me know.' She stood there waiting until the darkness had swallowed them up.

The speeding miles were white with moonlight. It was very crisp, the air sea-fresh with the incalculable excitement of the small hours.

'She doesn't like you,' Damian said almost immediately.

'Santegelo?'

'Who else? You make her feel crushed and lifeless. It's rather sad.'

Siri shivered.

'Are you cold?'

'No, Damian.'

His mouth was mocking and tender. 'How you say my name, Serena!'

They drove through one tree-lined avenue after another, a procession of shadows falling across the white sidewalks. A breeze stirred her hair.

'Wind the window up, Siri. I don't want you to catch cold.'

'I don't, you know,' she said lazily, watching a dilatory limousine.

His voice hardened. 'I didn't expect you to obey me. My intense passion for your voice hasn't blinded me to your faults.' He leaned across her and adjusted the window.

Not far from the house their headlights picked up a bizarre scene. Two men in dress clothes were hurling insults at one another, while their wives, and they were wives, carried on an amiable discussion.

'Civilisation going to pieces!' Damian smiled, and glanced over at her. There was silence in the unquiet dark.

Siri didn't wait for Damian to help her out of the car. She sped on ahead. The dew-wet garden smelt overpoweringly lovely. There was a gentle rush of wind through the trees overhead, scattering moisture. Siri's hand found the key under the mat.

.'Women!' Damian breathed beside her. 'They lock all the windows and they bolt all the doors, then they leave the front door key under the mat for anyone to find it.' He took it from her nerveless fingers and walked to the door.

Siri's heart was racing, its nervous thud loud in her ears.

'Don't dawdle, my lamb!' Damian's tone was light, purposely mocking, preceding the storm. He drew her into the darkened hallway, turning her towards him, her back against the door.

The whole evening had only been a prelude! ...

'And *now* ... *why* do you love me, as if you even know the meaning of the word!' His mouth was ardent. He drew her very close, feeling the fierce satisfaction of her slender yielding body against him. He spoke against her mouth with very hard directness. 'Has your fiancé kissed you yet, Serena? Like this ... or this!'

He gave her no opportunity to answer. A whirlpool of emotion spiralled out to her, drawing her into its dizzying vortex. She was submerging ...

His mouth trailed fire across her face. 'What sorcery is it, you smoky-eyed witch?'

She drew a long, shuddering breath. The tide of feeling between them was rising alarmingly. It was an explosive compounding of torment and desire. His hands on her bare shoulders were hard and hurting. The velvet darkness was charged with tension.

Siri moaned gently. Her mouth was a thousand-fold sweeter than she ever knew, as wildly responsive as even he could have wished. His own mouth was hard upon hers. There was no sound, no music, no laughter, only the pounding of her frightened heart.

He lifted her high in his arms. Segments of moonlight fell through the radial pattern of the skylight, showing her still, ivory face. Her eyes were closed, one hand pressed against her breast. He could feel her trembling, the feverish heat of her slender arms. But her eyes were closed to the inevitable enormity. The house was heavily quiet, almost as if it held its breath waiting for them.

'Siri!' He spoke her name in a low, swift voice. She opened her eyes, frightened by the intensity of her feeling for him. On a wave of pure sensation he bent his dark head and buried it in the silken column of her throat. The ring of the telephone cut into the darkness like a knife, restoring some measure of normality. Damian lowered her gently to the floor and walked to the downstairs connection.

His tone had reverted to normal, alert and decisive, with no shade of remembered urgency. 'Yes, Charlotte,' he said rather humorously. 'We've just arrived. No, nothing drastic.' There was a faint laugh in his voice. 'Yes, I'll tell her.' He hung up and found the light switch behind them.

The hall blossomed with light, spilling over her flushed cheeks, her tumbled hair, the unnatural brilliance of her eyes.

His smile was ironic. 'Saved ... in the nick of time! Charlotte is on her way. From the sounds of it, Mrs Morgenstern, sensible woman that she is, made as little as possible of the incident. I'd leave it go at that. Charlotte would only worry. I'll watch our Madelena,' He walked around, briskly flicking on lights, 'I can't wait for Charlotte. I'll get back and pay my respects to my hostess, then I'll call it a day.'

At the door he glanced at her. Her hair, black as jet, swirled about her face. His voice was completely level. 'Do something for me, child.'

'Yes, Damian?'

'Get rid of your fiancé. He cramps my style.' Then he was gone, walking out into the soft purplish light.

CHAPTER ELEVEN

FOR once, the positions were reversed. Charlotte slept on and on in the morning, leaving Siri to bring a breakfst tray about ten o' clock.

'Sit up, Sleeping Beauty.' There was no sign of Charlotte. The fleecy blue lambswool blankets were pulled up right over her head.

'Wakey, wakey!' Siri tried again to no visible effect, so she put the tray down and went to the Venetians, pulling them up with a vigorous clatter.

Charlotte's head emerged, swathed in palest pink chiffon.

'Awake, for morning in the bowl of the night has flung the stone that put the stars to flight.'

'Very likely,' Charlotte smiled and sat up, feeling for her coiffure. 'I was having the most heavenly dream.'

Siri's winged eyebrows shot up. 'Ah-hah,' she said, with heavy subtlety.

'No, really, it was about the bulb garden.'

'I'll believe you, thousands wouldn't.' Siri dropped two artificial sweeteners in Charlotte's tea and handed it to her.

'Thank you, darling. Such luxury!' Charlotte sipped her tea gratefully. It was a trifle strong, but then Siri never drank tea.

'Now you were very hazy last night. What really happened? I have my wits about me this morning, remember.'

'Just an unfortunate incident in an otherwise enjoyable evening. These things happen, Lottie.'

'I'd say they happen with alarming frequency when the Signora's about.'

'Perhaps,' Siri said noncommittally. 'Now tell me, who was that lovely man I saw you with last night?'

'As if I didn't try to introduce you! Lionised by this one and that one. I didn't think much of Greenwood's accompanying, did you?'

'Don't sidetrack, Lottie.'

'Gregory.' Charlotte tripped over the name. 'Gregory Kane. He was enchanted with your singing. I was so proud of you.' She reached over and patted Siri's hand, resting on the eiderdown.

'More, please,' Siri prompted, and settled herself more comfortably on the bed.

'Well, he's *the* Gregory Kane, the sculptor, and the most interesting man imaginable.' Charlotte was colouring, which was most unusual for her. 'He's Natalie Morgenstern's brother, did you know?'

'How could I, dear heart? But now that you mention it, there is a strong family resemblance.'

Charlotte considered for a moment. 'Yes, you could be right.'

Siri laughed. 'Oh, come on now, Lottie, you saw no one else. Admit it.'

'Do you think it foolish?'

'Lord, Lottie, the things you say! If he's *the* Gregory Kane, and as interesting as he looks, I'd say you'll have a great deal in common. Has he suggested showing you his chisellings?'

'Heavens, Siri!' Charlotte looked up, startled. 'Dinner was all that was suggested.'

'Ah-hah!' Siri said for the second time, conveying a wealth of meaning.

'Get out of here, Siri. I shall dress,' Charlotte said grandly. 'After another slice of toast, please, darling.'

Siri went out to make it.

By afternoon the rain had set in. so Charlotte curled up with a book, and Siri set about perfecting Act II of *Traviata*. She didn't hear the car for the downpour, and was surprised by the front door chimes. Clive stood on the porch, a very wet Clive, with rain cascading down his mackintosh.

'Clive dear, it's a wet day to come calling.' Despite herself, Siri was dismayed at the sight of his very wet shoes. The thought of them tramping over the new sapphire carpet was quite horrific.

'Would you mind waiting a moment and I'll get a mat,' she said apologetically. 'The new carpet, you know.'

Clive nodded patiently. He was used to the ways of women. Siri hurried back, placing the mat in a strategic position. Clive had already struggled out of his wet raincoat, placing it beside his umbrella on the white wrought-iron chair.

'Would you like me to take them off?' He glanced at Siri and down at his shoes.

'Heavens no, Clive, unless they're bothering you.

Women fuss, you know.'

Clive grinned. 'I do know, thank you—Just a moment dear, while I put this behind your head— no, not there, over there, Clive—not on that table, dear.' He mimicked his mother's quietly persistent tones.

Siri could imagine. She had never seen the Martyn abode even slightly untidy. It had an unusually unlived-in atmosphere. Then again, one had to eat and drink fast, because cups and plates were forever vanishing, washed on the instant and set down on the draining board. It was one of Mrs Martyn's most disconcerting habits, Siri decided, remembering the many cups of coffee, which she had set down inadvertently, to find whisked up in the next minute.

'Well now, I've come for a full report,' Clive said, and followed Siri through to the sun-porch.

'For the purposes of . . .'

'A quite burning curiosity.'

Siri smiled and settled back on the divan. Her crew-necked sweater was the same pale lemon as the wild roses that rioted over the contemporary print covering, her narrow-legged slacks the tan of the foliage.

'Do you do it on purpose?'

Siri looked quizzical.

'Pick your settings. Your outfit matches the divan.'

Siri glanced down at her tan slacks. 'My wardrobe is a trifle limited for that, but I do like to make the scene, as they say in the trade.' She drew her long legs under her. 'Now sit back, and I'll begin at the beginning . . .'

Siri had to admit that Clive was a good listener. His jaw dropped appreciatively when Siri came to Santegelo's display of malice. 'I say, how beastly, and how is the dress?'

Siri laughed outright. Clive was his mother's son. He said exactly what his mother would have said, and in the same tone of voice.

'A mess at the moment. I'll take it in to Farrow's first thing in the morning.'

Clive nodded his approval of her choice of dry-cleaners.

'By the way, I haven't had a chance to tell you my news. The Baroness had some very encouraging things to say about my accompanying.'

Siri sat up, swinging her legs to the floor. 'And why ever not? You're very good, Clive, very good indeed. Professor Engel always said so. Had she any suggestions to offer?'

Clive's face shone. 'Better than that. Letters of introduction. I haven't got them yet, but she has promised them to me. I think she's absolutely super! Hector Mainwaring was telling me she's helped many a young artist.'

'Well, what's holding you up, then, Clive? The sweet bird of youth is already on the wing.'

Clive moaned. 'Don't I know it! I'm twenty-five, you know.' For a moment he looked unpleasantly amazed.

'Come on then, Methuselah, let's go out to the kitchen. I've a mind to make scones.'

Clive got up at once. He was rather partial to hot buttered scones. His mother always made them when it rained.

'Talking to yourself, dear?' Charlotte's voice sounded relaxed and indulgent.

'Not this time, Lottie. Clive's here. I'm going to show him how to make scones.'

'Good, dear. I see no harm in that.' Charlotte drifted back into her book.

Clive settled himself into a kitchen chair and watched Siri go about making scones with a remarkable economy of movement. Surely she should be kneading them, or was that bread? He distinctly remembered his mother giving her scones several sharp pats before cutting them out.

'The red light is off,' he said in some surprise.

'Of course, Clive, the oven must be hot for scones.'

'I know *that*,' he said loftily, 'but isn't it rather soon? Mum's takes about ten minutes to get to the right heat and it's a new stove. I should know, I'm still paying for it.'

Siri confined herself to the dough. 'Set your mind at rest, Clive. I've been planning this all along. The stove has been on for a half hour.'

Clive relaxed. He had been told he was buying the best.

There were sudden footsteps on the path outside, a flurry of movement, then Damian opened the kitchen door, dark and glowing with scarcely a spot of rain on him.

His black eyes swept over them, lowering the

temperature. 'What a charming picture of domesticity! Our own sweet Siri with flour-streaked cheeks.'

'I'm quite sure I haven't.' Siri smiled at him, amused at his mood. It was obvious he was ruffled by Clive's placid presence.

'Why the tradesmen's entrance, Maestro?' She glanced at him, her eyes shimmering with mischief.

He turned on her. 'And risk running mud into the brand new carpet, darling,' he said with extreme sarcasm. 'Besides, it's much easier to run the car down the hill than trudge all over the house and garden.'

'Oh, quite.' She held his glittery dark look.

Clive moved uncomfortably. 'I was just admiring how deft Siri is. It's most unusual to find a musician so proficient in the kitchen.'

Damian's black eyebrows came together. 'Not at all. It's my experience that gifted people, women especially, have any number of strings to their bow. You could hardly expect their years of hard work and mental discipline to go for nothing in a different sphere. Nature is often unfair with her favours.'

'Why, thank you, Maestro!' Siri slanted a glance at him.

'I didn't say *you*, dear,' he said repressively. 'We have yet to try your scones, or is it a damper you're attempting?'

Siri only smiled, and slid the scones into the oven. 'In ten minutes you'll be forced to say *me*, dear.' She held his arms, stilling his restless pacing.

Clive's expression was staggered. Siri and

Damian St. Clair! It was unthinkable. His darling, sheltered Siri and the worldly St. Clair!

Apparently oblivious to him, St. Clair put out a hand, looping it through the thin black ribbon that tied Siri's hair. He pulled her towards him. In his face was tension and excitement. The silky curtain fell forward and Clive watched speechless as St. Clair wound a silky strand around his hand, drawing Siri inexorably closer.

Clive sprang to life, speaking with difficulty. 'I say, steady on, that's my fiancé.'

They both turned and looked at him with a uniform expression of surprise.

The Maestro's voice was mildly conversational. 'She may be your fiancée, Martyn, but she's completely under my thumb.'

'I say!' Clive repeated, at a loss for anything else.

Siri moved away from Damian. She had completely lost her bearings for a moment.

'If you'll just move your elbow, Clive, I'll set the table. It's so nice and warm in here.'

'You're joking!' St. Clair said sarcastically.

'Please, Damian!' She reproved him with her eyes.

'Are you sure you want me to stay?' Clive got to his feet.

'Clive dear, I've made easily a dozen of these infernal scones and someone's got to eat them. Now sit down and don't be silly.'

'Yes, do,' Damian added.

'Why don't you go along and say hello to Lottie, Damian?' Siri turned on him.

'Could that be something burning?' Clive asked fastidiously.

Charlotte suddenly appeared in the doorway beaming on all of them. 'Goodness, a tea party. Now what could be nicer! Damian . . . Clive. . . .'

'Lottie dear, Siri has just ordered me out of the kitchen,' Damian said. 'What do you make of it?'

'Surely not, Damian, but didn't I time it nicely?' She sniffed appreciatively as Siri opened the oven door and turned out the beautifully risen and, presumably, light-as-a-feather scones. She was rather precariously balancing the cake rack on the floor covered by a tea towel. Clive jumped up, meaning to make himself useful, as he always did at home, but instead startled Siri into losing her balance. For a split second her hand came in contact with the outside edge of the hot oven.

St. Clair reached her instantly, his dark face glowering. 'Now I've seen everything! You didn't burn yourself, did you, child?' He thrust the scones away from them and brought Siri to her feet, carefully examining her hand.

'No, of course not. Just slightly anyway, there's a red patch. Too many people in the kitchen, I suppose.'

Clive was incensed and mortified. Those two dark heads, one bent protectively over the other. 'I don't think I'll be able to stay after all, Siri. Mother will be expecting me. Excuse me, won't you?' He turned on his heel, making for the front door.

'Clive—!' Siri called after him. 'Could I get

past, please, Damian? We've hurt Clive's feelings.'

Damian continued to obstruct her way, his expression sardonic.

'I'll see to Clive,' Charlotte said quickly. 'Poor boy, he's *so* sensitive.' She went after him, catching him up in the hall. Clive allowed himself to be soothed. Charlotte was very good at it.

In the kitchen, Siri gave vent to her annoyance. Her eyes sparkled at him. 'You're rather cruel, Damian. I don't like to see people hurt. Especially Clive.'

'Don't you, now? Perhaps you'd prefer to hurt me.' His hand shot out, closing on her wrist.

'Why, yes, I would,' she agreed quite unfeelingly. 'Now that you mention it. You can look after yourself. Clive can't.'

He flung her hand away. 'All I have to do is keep calm,' he muttered, pacing the room like a caged panther. 'I can see what you need to be successful with women is the little boy lost look. The "please don't hurt me" ... "I'm too sensitive" ... pose. It's so much more interesting than a damned dull independent male!' He wheeled suddenly and put his hand to his temple with a grimace of pain.

'What's wrong, Damian?' Her voice faltered as she grasped his hand. She looked up into his frowning, dark face.

'My head,' he said irritably, reaching ineffectually for the back of a chair.

She drew it out for him. watching anxiously as he eased his long length into it. 'Rest for a moment, Damian. You've been overdoing it. You simply don't know how you drive yourself. Isn't there anything I can do for you?'

'Yes!' His black eyes flew open and his long arms pinioned her back against the table. 'Butter those damned scones!'

CHAPTER TWELVE

THE performance of *La Bohème* was very well received. Santegelo was in voice and, if her physical endowments did not suggest Mimi's fragility, her aspect and manner caught the true spirit of the appealing young heroine, locked in the grip of consumption. The performance and subsequent ovation had brought Santegelo right out of her irritable state of mind. She looked exhausted but happy.

The morning after opening night the critics were kind with a few reservations. The diva's unevenness of registers and occasional faulty intonation had not gone unnoticed, but, it was considered, that was more than balanced by her musical delineation and artistic insight.

Siri did not attend the lavish late supper arranged for the Italian prima donna and her colleagues, but those who did reported that Santegelo enjoyed herself immensely, eating and drinking with gusto until three a.m. with the result that, at the Wednesday rehearsals of *La Sonnambula*, her gowns were found to have shrunk.

It was thus to be expected that an aura of irritability hung over the rehearsal.

Siri sat alone at the very back of the stalls. It was best to keep out of sight. Santegelo's nerves were getting the better of her. Being a singer herself, Siri could actually feel the tension on Santegelo's vocal cords. Freedom and support were lacking.

Damian was maintaining a diabolical calm, his dark profile remote. The love duet was a fiasco, both singers so lacking in conviction that it almost amounted to a trial to listen to them.

Damian rapped on the music stand, bringing the orchestra to a halt. 'Would it be too much to ask for a little more ardour in the love scene? I find your big moment distinctly devitalising.'

At first it seemed as though everything would be all right. The small reprimand had called them to attention, but the tenor's closing phrase, an unusually beautiful and expressive one, came as the last straw to the soprano, so powerfully was it delivered.

'With what grief my heart is torn.' Julian Graham's splendid voice reverberated and without warning Santegelo flared into a colossal rage, slapping the incredulous tenor across the side of the head. It was a full-blown attack, and responded to in kind. The diva's left cheek was now correspondingly flaming red.

These manifestations of friendship, which flabbergasted the cast, were dwarfed by Damian's fury. He sprang on to the stage, his dark face satanic, pushed in his turn to the point of violence.

The diva was wheeling like a fire-fuming dragon, a wildness in her piercing eyes. Julian Graham stood biting his lip, his fume of anger spent. Damian advanced on the Signora, who, despite herself, fell back.

'If you could pay as much attention to your singing as you do to your histrionics, we could arrive at an electrifying performance, Signora. As for you, Julian, it's as well I believe in striking women. It's the only way to control them.'

'*Scandalo!*' the Signora screeched, finding full voice.

'Be quiet!' Damian thundered.

The theatre manager, unable to believe his ears, peered in through a side entrance, heralding a blast of cold air from the corridors. Damian's copious notes lifted like so many lost souls and scattered over the front stalls. Siri got up quickly to rescue them, whereupon the diva, misinterpreting her mad rush as an all-out attempt to usurp her, threw the first thing that came to hand—a bronze elephant which Julian Graham had been using as a paper-weight.

Siri swerved and ducked, but even then she was struck a glancing blow at the base of the skull. She came down the centre aisle.

'My God, someone get hold of that woman,' Damian roared so much with naked fury in his face that every voice was stilled on the instant.

It was no time for diplomacy. Julian Graham pinned the diva's arms, murmuring all the while, 'Steady now, steady,' much as one would a run away mare. The diva kicked him on the shins. The cast was treated to a blue streak of epithets. The situation was almost grotesque.

'Silence!' Damian thundered in open menace, and the Signora cut out. Damian turned and vaulted down to Siri. She was feeling the bump at the back of her head. His hand moved hers gently aside, assessing the extent of the injury for himself. 'You were lucky at that, it's not too bad. The sooner Santegelo is out of this business the better. Her nerves are all shot to pieces.'

'What about her victim's?' Siri questioned, feeling the bump gingerly.

Just to add to it, the diva broke into unrestrained weeping. Nothing could stop her tears, and no one was game to try.

Damian brought Siri to her feet, keeping one arm around her shoulders. 'Michael—' he summoned one of the young musicians, 'would you be good enough to drive the Signora home?' He looked directly at the diva. 'I suggest you try and get hold of yourself, Signora. You are allowing your furies to possess you. It won't be tolerated, I can assure you.'

Santegelo drew the tatters of her dignity around her. 'For now I shall retire,' she announced grandly.

'Splendid! Much the best thing you could do,' Damian replied.

The diva then swept off the stage like a deposed Empress with Michael in attendance. Damian waited for a moment, then addressed the cast. 'Ladies and gentlemen, your attention, please. Thank you. The details of this afternoon's storm, not as unusual as you might think, are nevertheless of interest to no one outside this theatre. You are entitled to your opinions, of course, but you have not my permission to express them, if you know what I mean.'

Laughter, nods and assenting murmurs came from the cast.

'Good. In that case, you may go. I know I can rely on your best for this evening.'

He turned to the long-suffering musicians. 'That winds it up for today, my friends. It's a case of each man for himself.' He leaned forward and said something to his first violin that brought forth a full-throated roar of laughter.

Siri had a pain in her head, and if that wasn't enough, she felt vaguely nauseated. She turned on her heel and fled up the aisle.

Damian caught her up swiftly. 'What is it, Siri?'

'Oh, please, Damian. I think I'm going to be sick.' She was desperate to avoid such a contretemps.

He put her into an aisle seat, holding her head down. 'Do you think I'd care, you foolish child?' He smoothed her dark hair. 'In a moment it will pass, and then I'll take you home.'

The manager appeared holding a glass containing a good tot of brandy. 'Would this help?' He passed Damian the glass, looking with concern at Siri's bent head.

Damian leaned down to her. 'Here, drink this, Siri. It should help. It smells like the best.' He glanced up at the manager, who positively smirked.

Siri drank it appreciatively and Damian laughed. 'So much for the coughing and spluttering women are supposed to do at the first drop of the hard stuff!'

'You'd wait in vain for me.' She smiled at him,

then looked up at the hovering manager. 'Thank you for sharing your best with me. Napoleon, wasn't it?'

'Quite right, Miss Linton. The bouquet alone usually brings my wife around.'

Damian handed him the glass. 'When you're ready, Siri. The car is at the back of the theatre. We'll go through the stage door.' He smiled at the other man. 'In case you're wondering, the curtain will go up as usual.'

The brandy on an empty stomach made Siri walk in a dream, the pain in her head subsiding.

Damian manoeuvred his way through the heavy inner city traffic and out on to the suburbs. After that, it was plain sailing. Neither of them said a word. Siri relaxed with her head tipped back, and her eyes closed. Sweet memories, stored away over the years, like honeycomb in its intricate cells, now flowed over her. She was drifting somewhere between reality and a dream state. She opened her eyes on yellow leaves shivering in the winter sunshine.

'Here already?' She sat up. He had parked the car on a wooded hilltop a few minutes' drive from the house. His hand came out, feeling for the bump on her head.

'Your first brickbat, poor child!' He drew her head back against his shoulder. 'Relax. Just shut your eyes and try to act like a normal civilised woman of the world.'

Her eyes flew open again. 'Coming from you, that sounds ominous!'

He settled her back into the curve of his shoulder. 'Soothe me, for God's sake. Isn't that what a woman's for? I'd like to think so.'

She smiled and relaxed, letting peace and contentment flow on unabated. 'I haven't the strength to stir,' she murmured after a few minutes.

There was a smile in his voice. 'Don't. This is where I want you for the moment.'

'Damian?'

'Umm?' He sounded rather abstracted.

'What do you suppose will happen to Santegelo?'

'Fiend seize the fiery lady!'

'No, seriously.'

His mouth relaxed slightly. 'There's nothing less conducive to my peace of mind than a question I can't answer. I don't know, Siri. And I don't care. Does that shock you?'

She turned her head slightly to look into his eyes. 'It was my head, you know. Why should it?'

'Well, you do have a look of compassion, my dove.'

'Common humanity, in this case. I've even read of rare cases of people literally going up in smoke. In the *Readers' Digest*, I think it was. Do you suppose that could happen to her?'

'What a remarkably level-headed observation,' he remarked dryly.

'I'm not making it up.'

'Be quiet!'

'Why do you stare at me like that?'

'Why should I not? You're beautiful enough, even with a bump on your head.'

She could see herself reflected in his sardonic dark eyes. The words came instinctively. 'You resent me, don't you, Damian? Some part of you resents me—the fiery male side of you. You can't bear for a woman to get under your skin. That would never do. It has to be the other way round. You're not going to be the one laid open to heart-ache like the rest of us. What *is* it you want of me?'

He shrugged, refusing to meet her eyes. 'I don't think I know myself.'

'You *do* know, and you won't tell me,' she accused him, warming to her theme.

He turned on her suddenly and caught her face between his hands. 'Don't talk any more!'

'But I ...!' Siri got no further, for he began kissing her young mouth, drawing a deeper and deeper response. Her head whirled softly around and around in an intoxicating dream, while her mouth told him everything she would not say. There was no one else in the world for her. Nothing so important as to have any meaning. Within his arms she had found a new world, iso-lated and wonderfully self-contained.

Here on the hilltop the wind was a symphony of sound, sighing, vibrating through the tall silver-trunked trees, like a million strings, each playing a different tune, but magically in harmony.

His mouth moved against hers. 'Tell me what you feel?'

She drew back a little. 'Frightened, perhaps, a little.'

'At least you have that much sense!' His mouth

curved ironically. 'And what of your career, Miss Linton? Weren't you going to be famous within five years? *This* won't help you. This floating around in a golden bubble.'

She was bewildered by the change in him. 'Don't you think I can be?'

'Of course you can ... if you keep at it. Unswervingly. Without distraction,' he said. The hard note in his voice was a warning.

Siri looked out at the clear blue sky. It was mild, almost warm. The soft golden days of spring were approaching. Nature -seemed aware of the over whelming beauty to come. The blue dome of the sky bent to the scented earth. It was bluer, clearer, the white drifts of clouds blown away like so much sea spray. There was a glorious freshness in the air. For the rest of her life, this afternoon was to come back to her, vividly over and over again.

'What are you really trying to tell me, Damian? That you would like to reject me? My personality? If so I know it already. You're too used to being all self-sufficient. It would be the devil's own job to commit yourself to a woman.'

His eyes were very dark and unfathomable. 'Whatever I feel, Siri, I have no place in my life for a camellia-skinned slip of a thing with some magic moving through her. You're too vivid, too vital. I'd have to take you right in with me to where I belong. It's a frightening feeling, one I've never entertained. My career has meant everything to me. And you have your own place to find.'

'But you have me captive, Damian,' she said almost desperately. 'You know that.' Her cheeks were flushed and her eyes were enormous. She looked at that moment terribly young and pathetic.

He drew a deep, exasperated breath. 'Why must you look at me in that particular way? You're so young, so romantic, so damned vulnerable. Sit up, I want no more nonsense. I'm taking you home!'

Charlotte didn't attend the performance that evening and neither did Siri, so they were not witness to Santegelo's most convincing role of the season. Twenty odd years ago, the Italian diva had sworn to serve her art in the best way she knew how, but nowadays, in her heart of hearts, she was humiliated by her too frequent outbursts, her complete lack of control.

The part of the captivating Amina had long been one of her favourites and she was determined to meet the not insuperable challenge of the main aria. And meet it she did, as Dr. Robert Greenwood testified in the morning papers.

But for that evening, Charlotte had a dinner engagement with Gregory Kane. Siri watched her dress, giving advice and a whole lot of extraneous comment. Charlotte looked very chic, in a black brocade dinner dress. She wore a double string of pearls around her throat and she was hesitating over a rather spectacular piece of costume jewellery for the lapel of her matching jacket.

'Too much like Woolworth's?' she asked Siri's reflection.

'No, I like it. You look a very stylish lady indeed.'

Charlotte's smile was pleased. 'Thank you, darling. My hair all right at the back?'

Siri got up from the bed where she had been lounging and got a comb.

'There you are. Just the ends flicked up. *Vive Steffi!*' The front door chimes sounded through the house. 'Heavens, that's your charming escort for the evening.'

The bells chimed again. 'That *is* my charming escort.' Charlotte almost panicked. 'Go down and entertain him, please, pet. I'm almost ready.'

Siri went through to her room quickly and collected her music case. With the house to herself she intended to practise. She skipped down the steps and opened the door with a flourish, sending sheets of music cascading all over the hall.

'It's only a wild guess, but I'd say you were a musician.' Gregory Kane bent down and helped to retrieve the copies.

Her gaze was very clear and direct. 'I'm Siri, you know.'

'Yes, I do know. I'm Gregory.'

His smile was as deeply attractive as Charlotte had said.

'How beautiful you are, Siri.' He spoke with uncomplicated admiration.

She took the last sheet from him, intrigued by his steady, curiously professional regard. 'Why, thank you, kind sir, but why the smile?'

'Your tone, my dear. The natural beauty's. With homage paid to her from the cradle.'

'And you don't approve?'

'Did I say that?'

They were smiling at one another as Charlotte came down the stairs.

'I like Mr. Kane, Lottie,' Siri said. 'He's very perceptive and surprisingly good at picking up a tune.'

Gregory smiled and came forward, taking Charlotte's hand. 'You look very elegant, Charlotte. Just the way I like a woman to look.'

Charlotte lifted her eyes and met his vividly blue ones.

'In fact, you're quite wonderful,' he said. 'In all sorts of ways.'

Charlotte coloured becomingly and said nothing, so Siri asked with interest in her voice, 'Would you two care for a drink before you go?' She looked from one to the other. 'Come on now, you're making me feel *de trop*.'

Charlotte burst into a warm, sweet laugh. 'What am I thinking of? Of course we would, darling. All three of us. Come through, Gregory.' She turned and smiled at him.

Gregory was looking around with interest. The chamois-coloured divan and deep armchairs were very effective with the sapphire carpet. The interior decoration had a sure, elegant, woman's touch that was like both of them.

'I like the house, Charlotte. It grows out of the site as surely as the trees. Who was your architect?'

'Well now, we're rather proud of him, aren't we, Siri? Noel Stricker is his name. He was only a student at the time, the very promising son of one of my clients. We were on a limited budget, but I think we have the best.'

'You have indeed.' Gregory glanced up. The soaring ceilings, on different levels, and great areas of glass, made the house seem a lot larger than it was and brought in the hillside vistas. An enormous brick fireplace faced the window wall, looking out over the wooded site. The night time sky showed through the clerestory windows and the silhouetted tops of the blue gums. It was a bold, contemporary, youthful vision.

'I know this young man's work. He won House of the Year for '69. The style has modified, but it's still unmistakable.' He looked over at the two women, who were giving him their full attention. 'I was trained as an architect. In fact, I spent ten long years at it. Hence the interest.'

'And ...' Charlotte pursued.

His powerful hand chopped the air. 'Oh, I wanted to be a free agent, develop my aesthetic faculties. The artist is never harnessed to utility, you know, the architect is to a certain extent. After all, you have to live in a house, you can't just look at it. The material needs have to be served. Let us say I was once bound to a form of conformity and now I follow my own inner force.'

'I think that calls for champagne, don't you?' Siri said admiringly. 'It just so happens we have a bottle in the fridge, awaiting such an occasion. Shall I get it?'

Charlotte smiled, 'Why not?'

'And it's such a beautiful night with all sorts of

possibilities drifting through it. That champagne seems in order.' Siri smiled at both of them and went through to the kitchen. She returned with the bottle and three glasses. It was cold and delicious and they had no trouble finishing it off.

'What shall you do, darling?' Charlotte looked round for her black sequined evening purse.

'Practise, as the old lady said when asked the way to the Town Hall.' Siri went on ahead and flicked on the porch light. The silvery crescent of the moon floated towards them through the dark rustling trees. 'What did I tell you, all sorts of possibilities!'

Gregory's face broke into an understanding smile. 'We'll think of you some part of the evening.' He smiled at her and drew Charlotte's fur about her shoulders.

'Perhaps I've stimulated your inner force. There's a head worth sculpting, or something along those lines,' she said pertly.

Charlotte looked up at her tall escort. There was no doubt of Siri's approval, and that was important to her.

'A significant silence, Mr Kane.' Siri looked over at him.

Gregory's eyes glinted. 'Maybe in a few years' time, when you're a woman,' he said, deviating from the truth.

'I'm suitably crushed, Mr Kane,' she called after them, as they disappeared into the garden.

CHAPTER THIRTEEN

DAMIAN had not called *Traviata* the eternal crowd-pleaser for nothing. Considerable interest had been shown at the box office and some enthusiasts went so far as to spend all night in front of the theatre waiting for the box-office to open. Scores of people were turned away on opening night, with the small comfort of being able to queue again for the next evening's performance.

Inside the theatre, every seat had been filled. It was one of the most brilliant assemblies of the year. Excitement and a glowing pleasure circled the theatre.

The German diva had arrived, resplendent, smilling and fervently applauded by her devotees. A small group of students had received autographs, a few gracious words and the admonition to 'work hard'. All society seemed to be there.

This was not to be one of those inspired musical evenings when everything clicks from beginning to end. Even so, Act I received a cordial reception. The scenery and costumes were gorgeous, the costumes especially, making every woman in the audience long to cut a dash for just once in a lifetime in one of those romantic period gowns.

There was a feeling that Santegelo was a trifle too plump, even allowing for the fact that one looks better on stage for a little extra covering. No one as yet was prepared to admit to disappointment. Out front, Damian was acutely conscious of the lack of fervour, the necessary throbbing anguish. He was doing his best and the orchestra was responding beautifully. But the trouble was Santegelo. With Siri, he was sure that he could have a triumph! The Italian diva was standing aloof from her Alfredo as she had done at rehearsals. He could almost feel their hostility. In his turn, Julian's characterisation was almost aggressive, his attitude far removed from the lover-like. And to make things worse, Mainwaring as Germont, Alfredo's father, was turning in the only ardent performance of the evening, constitutionally incapable of not playing up to an attractive woman. And Santegelo was still that! It was not until Germont's scene with his son that the required fatherly dignity and courteous restraint was apparent.

The 'Di Provenza' aria was the most effective of the night.... But by the end of the second act, it was obvious to the most uncritical admirer that the Italian diva was not playing the role to the hilt. Many of the audience were familiar with Garbo's *Camille* and felt let down. Garbo was Garbo, and not likely to come along twice in the one century, but even so. ... From one or two tentative moments in the first act, the performance steadily lost impact. And where was the acrobatic ease of the top register, the coloratura fireworks that had made Santegelo's name? Society patrons resisted the strong impulse to shift uneasily in their seats. The unsophisticates did not.

To the prima donna herself, the second act seemed interminable. When the curtain rang down she rushed back to her dressing room, calling for a hot drink to soothe her throat. Her dresser fussed around her, assisting her out of her beautiful afternoon gown and into the lacy white negligée and matching peignoir, appropriate to the last act set in Violetta's sickroom.

'Clumsy! *Senza finezza!*' Santegelo cried out in extreme and unfair irritation. 'Do I sound hoarse?' she questioned. 'My voice is lowering. I'm sure of it.' She tried a little quiet vocalising, then broke off abruptly. 'I can't go on,' she exclaimed hysterically, 'I'm ill.'

The dresser tried to speak calmly. The Signora was obviously becoming agitated. Her hands on the cup were shaking. She herself felt almost as tense. She couldn't ever remember such a highly-strung lady.

'The drink should soothe your throat, Signora, although your voice sounds quite clear to me. Perhaps you are imagining it?'

'*Dio!*' Santegelo set her cup down and gave a brittle laugh. 'Imagine it,' she repeated bitterly, and sprang to her feet. The sound of rending made both of them gaze down in speechless horror. The diva had put a good-sized foot through the fine lace of her peignoir.

It wasn't a catastrophe; it just seemed that way. Santegelo turned into a female ogre, roundly cursing the blameless dresser. To her credit, the little woman managed a firm silence. The uproar was heard through the thin walls of the other dressing rooms.

Damian St. Clair tapped on the door, then came in without waiting for the necessary entrée. He took in the situation at a glance, if indeed Santegelo was to leave him in any doubt of its seriousness. Marie, the dresser, hovered in the corner like a small, sad bird.

From then on, Damian became a pillar of support, seeing his production crashing round his ears. 'Do not distress yourself further, Signora.' He looked around the room, his eyes alighting on the Signora's own exquisite kimono of white-embroidered cream silk. 'This will do just as well. It suits you so beautifully. Your taste is superb.'

He held it out and quite unselfconsciously the diva slipped out of the torn peignoir and into her own garment.

'There, what did I tell you? Quite ravishing! In fact, too much so for our dying Violetta.' The diva still had a high colour, so Damian turned back to her dressing table and picked up a huge powder puff, whisking it over her face with an expert hand. His eyes met the dresser's over the diva's head. 'The Signora's hair, Marie—quickly now, draw it about her shoulders.' Marie hopped quickly to do so, while Santegelo was still standing as complacent as a small donkey.

With great theatrical flair, Damian took the diva's hand and pressed it to his lips. '*In bocca di lupo, Signora.*'

The small courtesy did a great deal for the diva's

morale. Though obviously shaken she returned to the stage trying to take a fresh grip on the role. The prelude to the last act was uneven. The quivering atmosphere of Violetta's sickroom was almost visible to the large audience. Upwards, upwards, from the divided strings, the frail pathetic music rose with the solo violin carrying the melody.

The curtain rose. The opera continued. But Santegelo's hysterical outburst at the interval, combined with her real or imagined illness, had a greater effect in sapping her strength than she had anticipated. Suddenly she threw her plump white arms in the air and fainted. Mercifully Violetta's sickbed was available. Stunned but undeterred, Hector Mainwaring reeled off several bars of improvisation. It was the only dignified thing to do. Then the curtain came down and stayed down.

Over the loudspeakers came the laconic announcement. 'Ladies and gentlemen, the evening's performance is ended. There will be no curtain calls.'

Out in the vestibule groups were forming with smiling faces and outstretched hands. Clearly Santegelo's faint, or in some camps 'plain refusal to get up,' had made the occasion. Gertie Howard, the commentator, was gleefully prognosticating an infinite variety of reasons for the diva's decline.

In another circle Jon Lawnton of a rival channel was keeping up a barrage of speculations and predictions on Santegelo's future. 'The last bid, you know ... got to squeeze some melodrama out of the thing ... risk everything on a last-minute gesture ....' The collapse, real or contrived, had seized the public's fancy. In fact, they all went home happier than might otherwise have been the case.

Backstage, medical attention was beginning to show its effect on the night's prima donna.

'How are you feeling, Signora?' A strange man was slapping her wrist. Without warning the events of the evening crowded in on her, causing her to turn her head aside in distress. The tears started. 'Now, now, my dear.' The slapping continued.

Santegelo tried to sit up and fell back again completely exhausted, her histrionic talent never more touching.

The doctor looked up at St. Clair. 'Nervous exhaustion without a doubt. The lady has been overdoing it, living on her nerves. I would suggest a week of complete rest. An extended period would be ideal. Her blood pressure is up.'

'A performance is scheduled for tomorrow,' Damian murmured.

'Yes, I know, but it's out of the question, unless you want a repetition of tonight.' The physician gave the pale woman on the divan another piercing glance. Her brow and upper lip were beaded with perspiration. 'All the signs of nervous exhaustion are there.'

Outside in the corridor there was a small commotion, then the Baroness von Richter entered the room, sweeping aside lesser luminaries with a flick of her sable stole. Santegelo was relieved and pleased to see her. She had never feared the Baroness. Von Richter radiated good health and balance and countless womanly attributes.

She lowered herself on to the divan, looking at her colleague with mock severity. 'But you have been overdoing it, my dear Madelana.'

The colour came into the Signora's face, and just as quickly faded. The Baroness was tender and gentle and quietly sincere, at the same time not unaware of the picture she made of golden munificence tending to a sick colleague.

'I *would* like to get my patient settled,' the doctor said, a shade testily.

The Baroness nodded mildly, then embraced Santegelo. 'We shall soon have you well again, Madelana, never fear. I shall see to it. A rest will be most beneficial.'

The Signora's eyes gleamed through their narrow-cut lids, then she broke into fluent German as no native could possibly have spoken it. The Baroness nodded two or three times, then the sopranos exchanged a last greeting.

Santegelo lay back among the cushions, giving herself up completely to the care of her medical adviser. For the next four days she languished in a quietly expensive nursing home, driving the staff to distraction.

Siri had watched the performance from out front, deeming it wise to keep out of sight of the Signora. She was given all the details of the collapse on the way home.

The realisation that she was to step into Santegelo's shoes burst upon her with stunning impact. Difficulties towered like mountain waves ready to engulf her. She saw Damian's beautiful dark eyes upon her and her face turned pale.

'But, Damian, I'm not ready! I haven't enough experience. No name, no background. *Non posso!* as the Signora would undoubtedly say. Besides, it would precipitate a nervous breakdown.'

'In *you*, dear child?' he asked, quietly sardonic.

'Of course not. Santegelo, she hates me.'

'Not *you*, Siri,' he stressed ironically. 'What you evoke. What she once had in some measure and must now say goodbye to.'

Siri was vehement defending her own kind. 'Well, I don't see why! Good grief, she's only about forty-two or three. How unfair it is! Why should a man have at least ten years on a woman?'

His mouth was mocking. 'Have you ever known a woman who doesn't think ten years a reasonable margin of error? I'd say Santegelo is closer to fifty. No one, least of all me, expects a prima donna to give her right age. No one would believe her, in any case. But that's not the point. It's *you* we're talking about. You're twenty-two and I say you're ready. Besides, if you haven't achieved international acclaim by the time you're thirty you'd better stay home and give lessons.'

Despite herself Siri laughed. Then she sobered. Damian said she was ready! What more could she want? Wasn't it always there, to shine like a deep, enchanted garden, awaiting the frantic beauty of blossoming? She experienced in retrospect the innumerable debuts she had made in front of her mirror. It was a familiar ever-changing scene. The brightest of bright hopes. One week Leonora, the next Violetta, and if she felt very bold—Norma or poor mad Lucia. Suddenly she felt sure of herself, a vessel through which could pour some magic alchemy.

'Vanity, vanity,' Damian said, watching her rapt profile. 'Have you made your decision?' They were both aware that the decision was out of her hands. This was her fate, what Nature had prepared her for, lavished such gifts on. Now she must accept the responsibility of those gifts.

Siri's voice became brisk, intent. 'You'll have to take me over my moves. What about costumes? Santegelo's won't fit. What do you think of my acting?'

Damian smiled in the darkness. She was already immersed in her role, all thought of inexperience, inadequacy, forgotten. 'You remember what Ellen Terry said?'

'Can't you see my round, wondering eyes? I can't.'

'She said, my dove, that the only time you are really acting on stage is when you are not speaking, for in speaking you are merely the mouthpiece of the author. The same applies to the singing actress to a large degree. One of our own great ladies of the theatre told me she had learnt a lot from watching the movements of singers to music. She herself liked to imagine music beneath her when she was on stage, filling in, accenting. . . .'

'Yes, I can appreciate that.' Siri's voice was pensive. 'Ellen Terry, Duse, Garbo. At least I saw

Garbo at a festival of old movies. Before that I used to wonder at the legend. Never after. I couldn't take my eyes off her.'

'Well, they won't be able to take their eyes off you by the time I'm finished with you. . . .'

Charlotte was waiting for them when they got home. She stood under the porch light, her face charming with welcome. 'How did it go?'

'Tell her, Damian.'

He was as bland and as innocent as a child. 'Over supper, providing it's a good one.'

'You'll tell me now,' Charlotte said, but stood back to let them in. She rested her back against the door, looking from one to the other. Her eyes lingered on Siri, appraising the wild rose colour. No, not wild rose, hothouse rose, gorgeous, scented, a satiny bud with the promise of the glory to come.

Siri couldn't stand it any longer. 'Lottie darling, prepare for a great surprise. I'm singing in *Traviata* tomorrow night!'

Siri looked and spoke so like her mother that Charlotte burst into tears, tearing into the kitchen in her distress. 'Live forever, lovely being dead. . . .' Damian found her there, came up behind her and turned her into his arms.

'Hush now, Lottie. It's an emotional moment for you, I know.' He kept stroking her hair, murmuring encouragements until Charlotte regained her self-possession. 'Now go splash some cold water on your face and I'll make the coffee. No more tears. Siri is crying her heart out. But it won't hurt her, she should sleep tonight.'

Ten minutes elapsed before the two women came downstairs again, smiling, their arms entwined.

Damian came forward, taking Charlotte's arm. 'I do so admire you extravagantly, Miss Frampton.'

A delicate flush mounted to Charlotte's cheeks at his obvious sincerity. 'A line here, funny if possible,' she said a little unsteadily.

'How about—speakest from the heart——' Siri came up with a quotation. They were still laughing as she poured the coffee. In her agitation she had brushed little exotic wings of hair out on to her cheekbones.

CHAPTER FOURTEEN

IN the years to come, those who attended the Saturday evening performance of *Traviata* were to boast of having seen the incomparable Serena Linton make her operatic debut. It wasn't a capacity house. The weather was unfavourable and an unknown young soprano was substituting for the Italian diva. To some, this was a combination of depressing factors. Yet it was beautiful out. The night was silvered with rain. It lay on the grass, glistened off the pavements, reflected light off the car tops and frosted with brilliants, the dark rustling trees.

Charlotte and Gregory hurried into the theatre between heavy showers. The pageantry of masks and manners was missing tonight! Everyone was too busy discarding raincoats and umbrellas, protecting their evening clothes. Charlotte was held in the grip of a kind of fearful excitement. It affected her throat, making her want to swallow constantly.

Towards curtain call the theatre started filling rapidly. They were mostly young people, students, those who would brave any kind of weather to see a performance under St. Clair. Quite a few were Conservatorium graduates, who had studied with Serena Linton and knew something of her talent. Clive Martyn was among them, a more confident Clive Martyn, with valuable letters of introduction in his case packed for London.

Out in the dressing room Siri was as white as a ghost and as silent. Madame Castelli had insisted on supervising her make-up and dressing. She moved about the dressing room with the methodical ease born of long years in the theatre.

St. Clair had not come in as yet. They had spent the morning going over her moves, which had to be reasonably close to Santegelo's so as not to throw the cast off.

The costumes had created a problem until the National Broadcasting had come up with Rowena Hartwell's. The English soprano had televised *Traviata* two years previously. They weren't as spectacular as the Signora's, but they were a good fit. That had been in the morning. By evening the wardrobe mistress had created a minor miracle with fresh flounces and glittering trimmings.

Madame applied the foundation. She had gone to great trouble, judiciously mixing colours until she came up with the one to enhance that lovely ivory complexion under strong lighting. The eyes were magnificent, carefully elongated and false eyelashes applied, the eyebrows lightly lacquered with a tube of French lotion. The elaborate hair-piece and additional curls added to Siri's own hair.

The make-up was done. She handed Siri a square of white cheesecloth, which Siri threw over her face to protect her make-up and dress. The dame then turned and took down the billowing gown of smoky grey satin in which Siri was to make her first entrance. She twitched the skirt into place, then stood back to admire her handiwork.

'*Bellissima*, Violetta.'

Damian came in smiling at Castelli. 'You are, and always were, an artist to your finger-tips, Madame. Serena has a great deal to thank you for.'

'It is so,' Castelli said modestly, and made a discreet exit.

Damian's eyes came to rest on Siri. 'Let me look at you.' His eyes travelled over every inch of her, seeking and finding perfection. 'Well, at least we've provided Julian with an exquisite love interest.'

He tipped her chin up. Her face was grave ... a little different under the heavy make-up, and her hands were icy. She was very still, very silent, her eyes as clear as a mountain stream.

'Listen to me, Siri. Tonight is not just *your* night. It's my night and Lottie's night and your mother's and your father's too. And Castelli's, and everyone who has put some part of themselves into making you what you are. What you will be. If you're uncertain, you only have to look to me. I'll always be there out in front of you. I'll never let you down. It's a promise even I can't escape.'

Siri turned back to her dressing-table. She took her string of pearls from its box and passed them to him. 'Do them up for me, please, Damian.'

He took the long string from her, one part of his mind admiring the flash of blue fire from the diamond clasp. Their eyes met in the brilliantly lit mirror.

Madame Castelli came to the door. 'Three minutes to curtain call, Maestro.'

'Thank you, Madame.' He touched Siri's cheek and went quickly from the room.

Madame hurried over. 'You will be all right tonight, *cara*. You have my word for it!' She pressed Siri's hand and drew her out into the wings.

And there Siri stood alone. Her heart hammering, hammering, with a totally new, sickening sensation. The heavy make-up tickled her skin. Nothing was real, the fantastic glare of the lights, the heavily painted faces of the cast, the stage, and beyond the curtain the sea of waiting faces.

Julian Graham came up to her, kissed the side of her cheek. Hector Mainwaring slid his arm around her waist. 'Good luck, love. You're so beautiful, you don't need much of a voice, but then you've got one, lucky girl.'

Outside in the street a spectacular clap of thunder followed by a great, jagged flash of lightning made itself felt in the theatre.

The curtain came up....

No one expecting to see a promising young singer and the protegée of the great Damian St. Clair could have anticipated the poetry, the passion and the magic of that evening's performance. After the first brilliant aria, a triumph was certain. The applause was spontaneous, deafening, holding up the action of the drama. The audience was lifted out of itself, their delight incredulous. Such beauty, such artistry, that fresh gorgeous voice, rounded sensuous, abandoned. She was an inspiration—and so young!

Under the impetus of her exciting original attack, Julian Graham turned in a glowing performance. This new Violetta had tapped some vital energy in him. The quality of silence that hung over the audience during the love duet was electric. The tenor's full, sensitive face, with its fine straight nose, and large lustrous eyes, was wonderfully ardent, while Violetta, released by his matchless support, soared above the orchestra, brilliant in her top register, velvety smooth ascending. A rare rapport flowed between the conductor and his principals. It seemed to Damian that she was anticipating his every wish. Siri was completely caught up in her role, no longer Serena Linton, but Violetta Valéry. Her interpretation was quite different from Santegelo's—youthful and strongly romantic, entirely credible.

When she suffered during the long last act, the audience suffered. There was such pathos, that peculiar veil of sadness in her voice. *'Gran Dio'*— 'To die so young!' She *was* young. She *was* beautiful and her Alfredo did love her. It was too sad for words. Before the final curtain rang down many damp cheeks were hastily dabbed. The ovation was shattering, going on and on, built up by the stamping of feet, the calls for Violetta.

Siri stood in the wings, swallowing rapidly, trying to hold on to her control. Inside, the tears were streaming down her. She needed Damian. The moment was too much for her. When he finally stepped on to the stage, Siri turned towards him and sank into a deep curtsey. The standing audience went wild as she turned and saluted them with the same moving grace.

The audience kept up the thunderous applause, the exact quality and temper of which Siri was never to experience again. The fierce pride, the belonging, the strong nationalism, the instant comprehension of greatness—it swept across the footlights in a tumultuous wave.

In the front stalls, Gregory Kane held Charlotte's hand firmly in his. Himself shaken, he was moved by her glowing face, stamped with pride and love and admiration. The unselfish years had paid great dividends. It was Charlotte's turn now to be cared for.

On stage Siri sank against Damian's shoulder, her great eyes shimmering with tears.

His voice was low, vibrant, meant for her alone. 'Look out at your future, my darling. *Our* future. These are our public, loving, admiring, devoted, demanding the best we can give them.'

Her heart lurched in triumph. Now at last everything was clear to her. 'You do love me, Damian. Don't try to deny it. Not ever again.'

He could only glance at her, brilliantly, briefly, with the applause tumultuous in their ears. 'With a love that moves the sun and other stars, Violetta! I swear there's no more to it than that!'

Be sure always to look for the name MILLS & BOON on the covers, so that you may be certain the books are genuine MILLS & BOON publications. In case of difficulty in obtaining the books—or if you would like us to send you post free our catalogue—please write to us:

MILLS & BOON READER SERVICE

P.O. BOX 236
14 SANDERSTEAD ROAD
S. CROYDON CR2 0YG, SURREY
ENGLAND

Will SOUTH PACIFIC readers please write to:

MILLS & BOON READER SERVICE

P.O. BOX 958
NORTH SYDNEY
N.S.W. 2060